The Storm Rises

The Solar Storm Saga, Book Zero

By Kyle Pratt

CAMDEN CASCADE
PUBLISHING

The Storm Rises

The Solar Storm Saga, Book Zero
A sidequel to the Solar Storm Saga
By Kyle Pratt

Paperback ISBN: 978-0-9983756-6-3
First edition – September 21, 2018
All Rights Reserved

Editor: Julie McDonald Zander
Cover Design: Inspired Cover Designs
Book design: Amit Dey

*   *   *

Sign up for my no-spam monthly newsletter and receive *free* ebooks, promotional offers, and discounts.

Details are at the end of the novel.

Acknowledgments

I admit at times I don't like writing, but I do enjoy that moment when I type the last sentence and know the book is finished. Yesterday I completed *The Storm Rises* and took the rest of the day off.

Today, I'm back in the office, but the exhilaration of finishing the nine-month writing process has not faded even though I'm not really done. Later this week, I'll take the final chapter to my critique partners, Robert Hansen, Kristie Kandoll, Barbara Blakey, Debby Lee, Carolyn Bickel, Joyce Scott, Pat Thompson, and Amy Flugle. They'll review it and I'll make edits based on what they say.

Next, the book is read by beta-readers Jennifer Vandenberg and William Childress, and I make more edits.

Then it goes to the editor, Julie McDonald Zander, and I make even more edits. These people who help me create books are both teammates and friends and I appreciate each of them.

I can't speak about my team without mentioning my wife, Lorraine. I couldn't write without her support and encouragement. Every chapter is read by her before anyone else sees it. She is my first editor, critique partner, beta-reader, and soulmate.

Thank you all for making this book possible.

Tomorrow, I'll start writing my next novel.

Prologue: Events on the Sun

Six storms churned on the sun. Over several weeks they grew to encompass an area fifteen times the size of Earth. Invisible magnetic lines of force danced, curved, and weaved above and between the storms. But on this particular day, as the magnetic fields bent and reconnected, a huge amount of ionized gas, called plasma, became trapped in the sun's atmosphere.

For the next few days, the plasma swirled and pitched in the corona region of the atmosphere, while it absorbed radiant energy and grew hotter than a nuclear fireball.

Finally, the superheated mass reached a temperature of more than ten million degrees Celsius and exploded as a solar flare. Much of it fell back to the sun, but, on the edge of the magnetic fields, several planet-sized clouds snapped like a whip, broke free of the sun's gravity, and hurled into space.

Astronomers call these plasma clouds Coronal Mass Ejections, or CMEs. Each possessed more energy than an entire year of the world's electrical production; these were hurtled at speeds faster than a bolt of lightning on a collision course with Earth.

*   *   *

If a disaster occurs you should be "ready to be self-sufficient for at least three days. This may mean providing for your own shelter, first aid, food, water, and sanitation."
Are You Ready? An In-Depth Guide to Citizen Preparedness
by the Federal Emergency Management Agency

But what happens on day four or five or ...

Day zero

Portland, Oregon, Saturday, September 3rd

A Humvee parked in front of his house couldn't mean anything good. Major Dirk Franklin sighed as he drove the last hundred yards to his home on a quiet residential street in suburban Portland. Two soldiers in combat uniforms with pistols on their hips stood next to the vehicle.

It had been a fun week of hiking, camping, and fishing with his oldest son, but apparently, the good times were over.

James leaned forward in the passenger seat. "What's going on, Dad?"

Franklin commanded the Portland Cyber Intelligence Center headquartered near the University of Portland. He could think of a dozen world situations that might bring a Humvee to his house, but in answer to his son's question, he said, "I don't know. We'll just have to find out."

"Maybe we should have brought our phones," James said.

"Maybe I should have, but you would have been talking to your friends the whole time." Despite the casual tone of his words, Franklin gripped the steering wheel tighter as he pulled into the driveway. He had hoped for a quiet weekend with his wife, Carol, before returning to work. That now seemed unlikely.

As Carol walked out the front door of their home, a sergeant stepped away from the Humvee.

Franklin strode to Carol, kissed and hugged her. Embracing her, he forced the concerns of the world to fade as he brushed her brunette hair aside and gazed into her hazel eyes. They kissed again and then he asked, "Do you know what's going on?"

"The news channels are talking about a storm on the sun, but the sergeant won't tell me anything."

"I'm going to call my friend." James hurried past them into the house.

"You mean Emma." Their youngest son, Logan, giggled.

1

Franklin ignored the boys and turned to the soldier now standing twenty feet away. The evening shadows were growing deeper, but still, he recognized Sergeant Keller, a trim, dark-haired man in his early twenties. As one of the soldiers who guarded the facility he had no security clearance, but Franklin decided to inquire anyway. He approached Keller and asked, "Is this about the solar storm?"

"Good evening, sir." Keller saluted. "All I know for sure is the colonel would like to see you as soon as possible."

Franklin sighed. "Okay, you can go. I'll be there shortly."

Keller stood fast. "I've been ordered to escort you, sir."

"Really?" Even during major network intrusions by enemy nations, command had never escorted him in. Franklin's gut twisted as he thought about the possibilities. "Why would they want to do that?" he muttered. "What's happened?"

The question had been rhetorical, but Keller answered. "We've received a few reports of unrest and some looting."

"I'll be right with you, Sergeant."

Carol shook her head and wrinkled her nose. "Take a shower before you leave. A clean uniform is on the bed. I'll pack some food."

*   *   *

Franklin walked into the operations center. Soldiers sometimes called it The Cube because each wall was nearly twenty yards long, making the room a huge square. However, this cube had ten large screens embedded in one wall, and twenty computer stations along a U-shaped work area. From here, a dozen technicians monitored and analyzed the flow of data along commercial phone, internet, and military networks in the region.

Today all of them, including the watch officer, Lieutenant David Poole, stared at a large screen where news commentators and analysts discussed the solar storm. Franklin had watched the news while dressing, but that provided only cursory information. He wanted details. "Everyone back to your stations. Lieutenant, come with me."

With Franklin in the lead, the two strode out the door at the rear of the ops center to an adjacent conference room. Franklin sat at the end of the rectangular table, allowing him to watch technicians in The Cube through a glass wall at the far end of the room. A whiteboard covered most of the wall behind him. A large political map of the world hung on another wall. "If a situation is bad enough that I get called in, I expect to find you managing it, not watching the news."

The lieutenant stiffened. "Yes, sir."

"Is the colonel concerned about the CMEs headed toward Earth?" Franklin leaned back in the chair. "Is that why he wants to talk with me?"

"Yes, sir."

"Are they large enough to cause an electromagnetic pulse?"

"Yes, sir. G4 or 5."

Franklin nodded. That would at least light up the night sky. "What's Norad, Strategic Command, and Vandenberg saying? I need facts before I talk with Colonel Sattler."

The door squeaked open and Colonel Don Sattler, a tall man with a full head of gray hair, walked in. "Franklin, I'm glad you're here. Has Poole briefed you?"

Not yet. Franklin cringed inwardly as he faced the colonel. All through his career, he had tried to know more than his boss about any situation, but today he felt like everyone knew more than he did. "The lieutenant is just getting started with his briefing."

Colonel Sattler took the chair next to Franklin. "Well, bring us both up to speed, Lieutenant."

"Four CMEs in the G4 or G5 range are—"

The colonel waved his hand. "I'm just an old soldier; give it to me in simple terms."

"A coronal mass ejection is essentially a magnetic cloud thrown from the sun at high velocity. These four are large and powerful." The lieutenant stepped toward the whiteboard and grabbed several markers. He scribbled a large yellow sun on one end and a tiny dot at the other. "Right now the plasma is hurtling toward the Earth." He drew four arrows in a line from the sun. "When these hit our magnetic field, the CME will compress the daylight side of the magnetosphere and elongate the night side."

Franklin nodded as he imagined the magnetic lines of force stretching and then snapping back as the cloud passed. If the CME pushed hard enough on the magnetosphere, the result could be catastrophic.

Poole's eyes widened. "And here's where it gets really interesting—"

"For now just tell me what it'll do to us," the colonel said.

"Yes, sir." The spark faded from his face. "Most scientists believe the first CME will release huge amounts of energy into Earth's magnetic field. About five hours later, a second one will repeat that, followed by a third a few hours later."

"What about the fourth one?"

"That one may miss or just glance along the Earth. We'll know more later if …."

"If what?" the colonel asked.

Franklin slumped forward, resting his arms on the desk as he contemplated how much energy four CMEs could discharge into the magnetosphere. It would be a long night.

"All that power surging in the magnetic field around the Earth will burn out our satellites." Poole strode along the whiteboard like a professor teaching a class. "It'll probably burn out the electrical grid worldwide. It could even destroy computer processors in everything from cars, cash registers, airplanes and even the controls for nuclear plants and hydroelectric dams like the one at The Dalles.

"We hardened? our equipment to protect it," Sattler said.

The lieutenant nodded. "And tonight that hardening will be tested."

"When will the first of these CMEs hit?"

"In about six hours."

*   *   *

Franklin discussed preparations and contingency plans with Lieutenant Poole as they walked through the building, inspecting induction shielding, circuit breakers, and grounding. "Do we have enough fuel for the generators?"

"Yes. The tanks are full and I told Sergeant Keller to fill up all the vehicles."

They were as ready as they could be. As they walked back to the conference room, Franklin worried about what might happen beyond the building, to society itself.

Poole turned left toward the conference room.

Franklin paused. "I'm going to call my family. If the colonel asks, I'll be there in a minute." Alone in his office, he sat behind his desk. Because of the shielding around the building, cellphones didn't work. He picked up his desk phone and tapped out the number for home. When he heard Carol's voice, he asked, "How are you?"

"I'm fine. How are you and how bad is it?"

"I'm okay. How much food do you have?"

"Enough for six or seven days."

That was more than FEMA recommended and more than they had ever needed, but on this night it felt inadequate. "Try and buy more supplies." Thoughts of panic buying flashed through his mind. "But take James with you and stay safe." Those words felt hollow and meaningless. "I love you."

"I'll be fine. I love you, too."

Moments later, as he entered the conference room, Franklin made a mental note of those around the table. Colonel Sattler had moved to the head position. Local directors and managers for DIA, DHS, CIA, and other alphabet agencies filled most of the other seats around it. Poole, along with a dozen others, sat along the wall while several clusters of civilians argued nearby.

Franklin sat in his usual chair beside Colonel Sattler.

The colonel wrote on a yellow legal pad for several moments and then stood. "Gentlemen, ladies, the first cloud hits in five hours. Before then, we need a plan to protect our equipment and accomplish all, or at least most, of our various missions."

"The only way to be certain the equipment is protected is to disconnect from the power grid and the network," Franklin said.

"You can't do that." Anger creased the face of the local FBI agent in charge. "We have an agreement to use this facility on a continuous basis—*continuous*. We need your network up and available for several ongoing criminal investigations."

"We're tracking hacker probes into DOD networks from several countries," another civilian added. "We've got to stay online."

"Did you two fail high school science class?" Lieutenant Poole stood with his face growing deeper shades of red by the second. "This could be catastrophic."

Franklin motioned for him to sit. "The lieutenant makes a valid point. If we don't shut down, our equipment might be seriously damaged. We could be offline for weeks after that."

"If the solar storm causes that much damage, there won't be a functional power grid or internet," the local NSA chief snarled.

Sattler leaned toward Franklin and raised an eyebrow.

"I think we need to shut down," Franklin said. "Several agencies including NASA, NOAA, and the Space Weather Prediction Center are working to provide us with accurate impact times. We should shift to emergency power about an hour before the storm arrives and then shut everything off."

A sergeant hurried into the conference room. "Excuse me, Colonel; General Abbott from Cyber Command wants a video conference with you."

"Project it on the whiteboard, Sergeant, and erase those arrows."

When General Abbott's image appeared, Colonel Sattler stood and faced the camera above the whiteboard. "General, I'm here with my staff and stakeholders. Does this need to be private?"

"No, Colonel, they should hear what I'm going to say. The president has declared martial law. You are hereby promoted to the rank of brigadier general for the duration of the emergency. We are still hoping there will be no significant disruption of command and control authority. However, if you do lose contact with the chain of command, you are to assume control of all military forces, law enforcement, and Coast Guard personnel within your operations area."

"Yes, sir."

A lieutenant stepped into view and whispered to Abbott. The general nodded and said, "I have to go. Good luck and Godspeed." The screen went blank.

Colonel Sattler leaned his head back and stared at the ceiling for several moments. "How fast can you shut down the classified network?"

"It's easier to take it down than bring it up." Franklin rubbed his chin. "Fifteen minutes from full operation to completely down."

"How fast can you return to normal operations?" the colonel asked.

"If the power and networks outside the building remain up and stable, we can be back to regular operations in less than an hour."

"Then that's what you have, Major. Fifteen minutes before the first CME hits take the classified network down and shift to generators. Then we'll use the unclassified network to monitor the situation. If we remain in contact with command authorities I want secure operations restored in one hour."

"Yes, sir." Franklin cringed and wished he had given himself more time.

*   *   *

Franklin slammed the receiver down on his desk telephone. Since telling Carol to get more supplies he had called her cell phone and the house a dozen times without success. He looked at his watch. The night might still be young, but they were out of time.

He strode from his office and down the hall to the ops center. As he entered, he glanced at his watch and then the red digital clock high on the wall. "It's time. Take it down." Six soldiers fanned out through the room, shutting down computers.

Everyone should have been ready, but four civilian technicians continued to work until the last possible moment, grumbling complaints as they did.

Franklin was not in the mood to hear any arguments. He ignored them and remained stoic at the back of the room near the door. This had always been the best view, but tonight there was little to see. In quick succession, every screen flickered off and the usual hum of activity faded.

The civilians grabbed their coffee cups and left the room.

From the watch desk, Lieutenant Poole dialed his phone. "Shift to backup power."

Lights flickered and then returned to normal in The Cube, but in the hallway, only emergency lights shone.

A few minutes later, a private darted into the ops center. "The unclassified network is down. We don't have comms with anyone."

Poole picked up the phone, but this time shook his head. "No dial tone, sir."

With flashlight in hand, Franklin walked through dim corridors, checking offices like a night watchman making his rounds. The glow of emergency lights cast ominous shadows along the halls.

He didn't know what he expected to find, but the walk around the building lent him some comfort. Power remained out, but everything else seemed normal. Eventually, he reached the main entrance.

Sergeant Keller saluted him. "Good evening, sir. Have you seen it?"

"Seen what, Sergeant?"

"The lights." Keller motioned for Franklin to follow him outside. "See?" He waved at the sky.

Ribbons of red, green, yellow, and purple weaved across the sky like oil on dark water.

"And do you hear it, sir?"

"I don't hear anything."

"Exactly."

Franklin nodded as understanding hit him.

Silence had overtaken the city.

Day one

Portland, Oregon, Sunday, September 4th

"Inside this building our equipment has been protected from the CME." Sitting in the conference room, Major Franklin frowned as he tried to imagine how the people of the city would react when they woke to no power, water, or communications. "Beyond these walls, we have very little information. We need to know what happened to get an idea of what will happen over the next few days and weeks."

"I'm sure the electromagnetic pulse burned out most modern technology worldwide." Poole leaned his elbows on the table. "Several pulses, probably. A lot of people are going to die."

Poole sat directly across the conference table from Franklin. A single LED lamp between them left most of the room in darkness and cast deep shadows on the lieutenant.

"You're right, Major, we need facts." General Sattler stepped from the blackness into the gloom.

"We know that commercial power is out along with internet and military networks," Poole said.

"But this might be a localized problem," the general replied.

Poole shook his head. "I doubt it."

Sattler strode to the head of the table. "Major Franklin, if Lieutenant Poole is correct, we no longer have a Cyber Intelligence Center and we won't for a very long time. What I need now are real-world facts. At dawn, take Sergeant Keller along with two of the security squads and, if needed, add some of your specialists. Then investigate the local situation. If power and communications are out across Portland, go to Salem. Advise the civil authorities of the situation, and then report back here."

"Yes, sir. Shall I also check on unit families in the area?"

"Good idea." Sattler nodded. "I'll handle those close to base. You check on the ones farther out. Also, bring water and extra food from our stocks."

Franklin nodded. This was a mission he would gladly accept because the family checks would include his own.

*   *   *

Standing in a shadow, Franklin zipped the jacket of his Army Combat Uniform jacket a bit higher and then strapped on a holster for the first time in many years. He watched an orange sun climb over the hushed city of Portland. It seemed as if the entire world held its breath, waiting for answers.

In the distance a lone dog barked.

Medic Karen Bickel lugged a large pack of medical supplies toward one of the trucks. Franklin hoped she wouldn't need them.

Sergeant Keller jogged over to him and saluted. "I've secured the supplies you ordered along with four vehicles, two Humvees, a fueler, and the deuce-and-a-half truck with that plow blade you wanted. We've been working on the cars but can't get any to run."

"What's wrong with them?" He felt foolish for asking.

Keller shrugged. "The dash lights come on, the windows even go up and down, but the engines don't turn over. They just click."

"The CME probably damaged the computer processors." Franklin's jaw clenched. If the storms inflicted that level of damage on their cars, what would he find as they traveled through Portland? "Ensure all the men are armed, Sergeant."

"Yes, sir.

"Okay, Sergeant, when you're ready, lead with the deuce and have Braun ride shotgun." Franklin reached into his jacket pocket and retrieved a handheld transceiver and a paper. "Take these. The paper is a map of our route. The radio was in our building so it still works. I've got one and I'll get more for the other drivers. Any questions?"

"Yes, sir." Keller pointed to the map. "I understand the stop at the airport and city hall, but there must be twenty other stops marked all over the city of Portland. What are they?

"Twenty-two stops, Sergeant. We're checking on unit families. You'll see your address noted on the side of the page."

Keller ran a finger along the paper. "Thank you, sir. Also, why did you want the plow blade on the truck?"

"Clear the way for the convoy, and keep us moving."

Keller raised an eyebrow and grinned. "Yes, sir."

"I'll be in the Humvee right behind you."

Atop the flag pole the stars and stripes fluttered in the cool breeze as Franklin exited the building with additional radios. He shivered as he handed the first one to a driver. When finished, he climbed into a Humvee with Private Scott Thomas. "Do you have family in the area?" he asked.

"No, sir. I'm single. My parents live back east."

Franklin nodded. He hoped that Thomas would see them again, but he doubted that opportunity would arise anytime soon. Clicking the radio, he said, "Head out."

As the convoy pulled from the parking lot, the deuce slammed into an abandoned car and pushed it aside with the plow. Franklin grinned. Keller would have a memorable day.

After the deuce banged past a couple of more vehicles, Franklin clicked on his radio. "You don't need to smash into every car on the road, Sergeant, just the ones in the way."

They crossed under a silent freeway and for the next half mile the convoy weaved around abandoned cars as it followed along quiet streets. Most homes and businesses appeared untouched, but then the convoy passed a burned-out strip mall. Shards of glass sparkled across the parking lot in the early morning light.

Abandoned cars and trucks filled the intersection just ahead. The screech of metal on metal resounded as Keller plowed a path through. Two blocks beyond, the convoy turned down a residential side street. Curtains pulled back and people gazed from dark homes as the rigs stopped in front of an older blue two-story house.

A woman stepped out and walked to the middle of the yard.

Franklin glanced at the list for her name and then joined her on the lawn. "Mrs. Gray, we're doing welfare checks on unit families. How are you doing?"

"I'm fine." She let out a worried breath. "I watched the news until the power went out. Is Jake okay?"

"He's fine. Do you have enough food and water?"

"I do for a couple of days. When will the electricity and water be back on?"

He had little hope that the utilities would be functioning anytime soon but said, "We'll be checking on that today."

At the second home, Franklin spoke to a man whose wife served in the unit. He asked similar questions and received similar answers.

After several other family checks, the convoy drove through an older part of the city. When the vehicles stopped, a pregnant woman walked out of a small Craftsman-style home.

She asked about her husband, electricity, and receiving supplies from one of the trucks. Then she inquired about the nearby hospital. "Is it still open? Can I have my baby there?"

"We'll check." Franklin glanced at his map. "That's our next stop."

Older wood homes and brick buildings surrounded the modern steel-and-glass hospital. Men and families walked up and down the streets, but few women walked alone.

As he stepped from the Humvee near the hospital main entrance, the first thing Franklin noticed was the sound of engines. Generators? Perhaps the hospital remained operational.

The smell of diesel fumes and wood smoke hung in the air.

"Sergeant Keller, stay here and guard the vehicles. I'll take the medic and a couple of armed soldiers and check the hospital."

"Yes, sir."

Pungent smoke hung unseen in the air as they approached the agitated crowd that blocked all view of the main entrance.

"Make way," Franklin said as he edged his way into the crowd. "Stand aside."

"How come you get to go in? We need things too," a man on crutches said.

Franklin ignored him and pushed on with the other soldiers.

An even larger crowd, some in wheelchairs, others with walkers or crutches, packed the lobby. Just in front of him a man with a towel around his arm dripped blood on the floor. Several children and babies cried.

Franklin and the soldiers pushed their way through to the counter. Three women attempted to direct patients to doctors, nurses, and wards.

After watching the turmoil for a moment, Franklin said, "I'd like to speak to the hospital administrator."

The nearest woman scowled and threw down her pen. "So … would … I." Her face grew redder with each word. "Through there." She thrust her hand in the direction of two security guards blocking the way to a nearby hall. "Fifth floor, room 515. You'll need to use the stairs. The elevators aren't working." The woman stood and shouted. "Bill, let these soldier guys go through."

As Franklin strode down the hall, he felt comforted by the glow of fluorescent lights above. He pushed open the stairwell door. Above, doctors and nurses hurried up and down illuminated flights.

The three soldiers joined the climb. Sweat beaded on Franklin's forehead when they finally pushed open the stairwell door on the fifth floor. He put his hand on a nearby vent. The air felt warm.

When they reached the office, Franklin knocked on the door, opened it, and entered.

"Who are you?" The man behind a large desk jumped to his feet.

"I'm Major Franklin on a fact-finding mission for the area commander." He held out his hand and they shook. "You're the hospital administrator, correct?"

"Yes. My name is Emerson Montgomery. Please sit down." He pointed to chairs and everyone sat. "Normally I'd ask how I could be of help to you, but today I'd really like to know if you can help me."

Franklin shook his head. "We won't be able to assist you today, but tell me about your situation and we might be able to get help in the days ahead."

Emerson sighed. "We have generators, but everything … MRI, X-ray, ultrasound, heart monitors … everything is down. Also, the toilets don't work … there's no water. Dysentery … hepatitis … e-coli … we're going to have a huge problem very soon. "

A drop of sweat ran into Franklin's eye. "Does the air conditioning work?" he asked as he rubbed his face.

"No. Ventilation is functioning, but not cooling or heating." The administrator shook his head. "When will power and water be back on?"

Franklin had no answer, but knew it wouldn't be soon. "Conserve fuel for the generators, triage your patients, and post an armed guard in the pharmacy."

Color faded from Emerson's face. "So, it's going to get worse?"

"I think so." Franklin bit his lip. "Make a list of your most urgent needs and give it to Corporal Bickel, our medic. That is the best I can do today."

As Franklin left the hospital and walked back toward the vehicles, gray smoke hung heavy in the air. He unfolded his map and looked for their next destination.

Keller hurried to him with wide worried eyes. "There, my home. That's next," he pointed. "We've got to go. Now!"

Franklin followed his gesture. Smoke rose from a white wood-frame apartment building a couple of blocks away. "Why didn't you say your home was on fire?"

"I just spotted the flames." Keller continued to stare at the burning tower.

"Mount up," Franklin ordered. "Let's go!"

The convoy arrived in less than a minute. The lead vehicle lurched to a stop. Keller jumped out and pushed through the families clustered along the sidewalk. Ash drifted in the air from orange and red flames that had blackened one side of the building and continued to burn up the wall. The charred ruins of dozens of homes scarred the landscape for blocks beyond.

"Stay here and guard the convoy," Franklin shouted to the others as they jumped from their vehicles. Then he followed Keller into the burning building.

Franklin coughed and his eyes watered as he scanned the lobby. Only a few people hurried down the stairs, and they darted through the smoky lobby like ghostly specters as they hurried out. Franklin held the page close and read the apartment number. Somewhere in the smoke above him a baby cried. He started up the stairs.

"Major, sir, I'm here."

Keller, burdened with suitcases, hurried down the stairs with his wife, Katie, and their baby. Handing the cases to Franklin, Keller said, "Please take these, sir," and disappeared up the smoke-filled stairwell.

Eyes wide with fear, Katie stared in the direction her husband had gone.

Anger gripped Franklin as he choked on the smoke and struggled to inhale. Had Keller returned to the fire to get more from his apartment? "Let's get your baby out of here," he said to Katie. "Then we'll find your husband."

Outside, he pointed to Privates Kohen, Rankin, and Thomas. "Go to apartment 214 and get Keller. Drag him out if you have to."

The three disappeared into the growing clouds of smoke.

Families crowded around the convoy, seeking answers.

The soldiers couldn't provide much information, but they handed out water bottles to all who asked.

Katie opened one, drank deeply, and then washed her infant's face.

Bending at the waist, Franklin drew in a deep breath. Then he drank, coughed, and spit. When able to both breathe and see, he focused on the lobby entrance. Why had Keller gone back?

Smoke billowed as the door swung open. A soldier stumbled out and fell to his knees, coughing. The medic ran to his aid as a second and then a third soldier emerged from the burning building.

Franklin hurried to the soldiers he had sent in as others provided water. "Where's Keller?" he asked the men kneeling near the entrance.

One of them pointed back inside.

Franklin's gut churned. During his career he had lost several men under his command. He didn't want to lose another to a fire.

Two forms emerged from the smoke. As they slumped to the concrete steps, Franklin recognized Keller and a woman holding a baby.

The mother coughed and gagged. Still struggling to breathe, she jiggled the baby. "No … no."

The infant made crying motions, but no sound escaped. Franklin felt helpless. "Medic!"

Corporal Bickel took the child and thumped it on the back. The infant whimpered and then wailed.

Still holding her baby, Katie ran to her husband with water for him and the woman.

Franklin turned to Keller as he poured the water on his face and then drank.

"Why did you go back in? Is that woman a friend?" Franklin asked with growing irritation. "Is that why you went back?"

"No, I heard the baby crying when I came out of the apartment. I had to try to find them. Is everyone out?"

"I sure hope so." Franklin's ire softened. "I'm not sending anyone else in. Load up your family and things in the truck." He allowed a weak grin. "We'll pin a medal on you later."

An angry inferno now consumed the upper stories of the apartment building.

"Mount up," Franklin ordered. Over the radio, he said, "Drivers, we're leaving in one minute."

"What are we supposed to do?" a man shouted.

Franklin stared at the desperate and now homeless families as he struggled for an answer. "Go to the nearest fire station." Would anyone be there? They hadn't responded to this fire. "Maybe the Salvation Army or one of the other local churches." The words sounded callous and hollow, but what could he do? His resources were limited and he held out little hope of resupply. Looking out at the blocks of charred rubble, he worried about Carol, James, and Logan. Were they now homeless—or worse?

The convoy drove along several burned-out streets and then reached a major boulevard that had acted as a firebreak. Seeing the unharmed homes beyond, Franklin inhaled a deep breath and prayed that his family had been spared.

Keller and his plow blade swept several cars aside as the convoy crossed from blackened ruins into a typical residential neighborhood. Every night Franklin drove this way, past familiar homes, to his own house, and this portion had never taken long, but today the Humvee seemed to only inch forward. He forced himself to sit still and breathe as they passed the last couple of side streets.

When the convoy turned down the road toward his home, Franklin smiled with relief. The entire street appeared unscathed.

Several people stepped out and watched as the convoy slowed. When the vehicles neared his home, Carol hurried onto the porch with Logan.

Franklin jumped out and nodded to Ted, his nosy neighbor, watching from his kitchen window.

"We've got to stop meeting like this." He hugged Carol tight and, despite regulations, kissed her. Then he hugged Logan. "I've been worried about all of you. Where's James?"

"He went to check on a friend."

"Emma." Logan snickered.

"The next block over." Carol pointed.

"Do you know her parents?" he asked.

"I haven't met them yet," she said. "James doesn't think I know about her."

"Shouldn't we … maybe be a little proactive?"

"You mean me, right?" Carol locked a firm gaze on him. "Emma's father is a police officer. I figured I could wait and see if it grew into anything."

"Okay." Franklin nodded and relaxed a bit. "I'm just saying *we* should keep the boys close. How are you doing?"

"We're fine now." Carol shook her head. "But you smell like smoke."

Franklin explained what had happened.

"Did you see the fire, Dad?" Logan asked. "It was huge!"

"I saw some of it and the burned homes." Franklin turned to his wife. "The thought of it reaching you scared me."

Carol nodded. "We were packed and ready to run if the flames drew close. How are you doing?"

"I'm fine. We're out trying to assess current conditions."

"I was still watching the news when we lost power. How bad is it?"

"We still need to check the airport and then head downtown to city hall and police headquarters, but it's looking like the EMP affected at least the metro area."

Carol shook her head. "It wouldn't be just here."

Several times during the years of their marriage, he had tried to hide the full truth of troubling events from her, but she always seemed to know. He nodded. "It's probably worldwide, but we don't know yet."

They talked for a few minutes and then he asked, "Were you able to get more food before the power failed? How much do you have?"

"I got some, but people were in a panic ... buying everything. I've got eight days maybe. Ted's been talking to the neighbors. Word is that none of the nearby stores are open and some have been looted."

Franklin could imagine the looting and didn't want Carol near it. "Don't try to buy more. If you need anything, go to the Intel Center."

"The car doesn't work. How would I get there? On a bike?"

He frowned. His home was a short fifteen-mile commute in a car, but now most vehicles didn't function. Those he loved were on their own until he could return. "Keep the guns loaded and ready. I've got to go to Salem and report, but I'll be back at the Intel Center by tomorrow morning, long before you run out of food."

Minutes later, the convoy climbed an onramp to the freeway. From this vantage, Franklin spotted several columns of smoke drifting high into the still air. Only a few motionless cars and trucks dotted the freeway, allowing Keller to increase speed as he led them toward the airport.

On the far side of the freeway, a man pushed a shopping cart filled with suitcases.

"Look at all those people around that church." Private Thomas shook his head.

"Eyes on the road, Private." Franklin continued to stare at his map. What could a church do at a time like this?

"Where do you want me to go when we reach the airport?" Keller asked over the radio.

Franklin shrugged at the device in his hand and pressed transmit. "Arrivals."

Clusters of people stood along the road near baggage claim. If not for the lack of vehicle traffic, it might have been a normal day. The sidewalk crowd moved toward the convoy as others scurried out of the terminal. Seeing the mass of civilians caused Franklin unease as the vehicles rolled to a stop. Again, he pressed transmit. "Drivers, stay with your vehicles. Soldiers, deploy with your rifles." Then he stepped from the Humvee as the crowd swept toward them like a wave.

"Are you in charge?"

"When are flights resuming?"

Without a word, Franklin strode into baggage claim surrounded by his men. Light shone through windows and from fixtures above. The airport had at least some power. Cots, burdened with weary passengers, lined the walls on either side of the baggage turnstiles.

A police officer ran up to the soldiers. "Are you here to relieve us?"

"No." Franklin shook his head as he stepped forward. "We're checking on the situation in the Portland metro area. What's the status of the airport?"

"Closed," the police officer said with a frown. "Well, sort of. Last night, after the final plane landed, the Port Authority closed the departure terminal, but a lot of people weren't able to leave before the power went out. Then cars and buses wouldn't start." He shrugged. "Eventually, they got some power back on, but radios, phones and computers aren't working. We got the cots and blankets out of storage." He pointed to several police officers and TSA agents who had joined the growing swarm around them.

"Where's the manager?"

"I have no idea," the police officer snarled.

"Why aren't there any flights?" a woman in a gray business suit shouted from the growing crowd. "Is FEMA working to restore power?"

A man in shorts and a Hawaiian shirt pointed at Franklin. "Are you in charge?" He pushed to the front of the crowd. "I need to get to my family."

"Stand back," a soldier ordered.

Other soldiers moved to block his way with rifles at the ready.

"I missed my flight," a woman with two small children said. "We live in Atlanta. How can I get there?"

Franklin stood on a chair and looked over the growing crowd of confused, tired, and angry people that now encircled them. What information or guidance could he give them? He held his hand up and the questions hushed. "The president has declared martial law. The electric grid appears to be down throughout the city and possibly worldwide. Until communications are restored, no civilian flights will be departing." He didn't know that for certain but couldn't imagine a civilian aircraft going anywhere without air traffic control.

"When will power be restored?" another man shouted.

"We don't know. You'll need to provide for yourself for the next three to five days ... perhaps longer."

A gasp rippled through the crowd. Several adults and children cried.

"Are you kidding me?" a man in a dark business suit and red tie bellowed. "That's not good enough. My car won't start. What do you expect me to do? Walk to a hotel or restaurant?"

"Well, you could." But Franklin doubted any of those were open.

A few people asked questions, but more shouted them. Others screamed angry curses.

Realizing the mob might turn violent at any moment, Franklin stepped down from the chair. "Fall back and mount up." He clicked transmit on the radio. "Drivers, we're leaving ASAP."

Soldiers pushed back through the crowd as the Humvee engines rumbled.

Several men pressed against the soldiers.

A man struck Private Parson on the jaw. Parson hit him with the butt of his rifle. The man stumbled backward and then dropped to the floor.

"There are a dozen people standing in front of the deuce." Keller's worried voice blared over the radio. "I'm not sure they'll move."

"Push through, Sergeant," Franklin replied over the radio as he opened the door to his Humvee.

"Are you sure, sir?"

Franklin nodded at the radio. "Very sure." He slammed the door shut.

A gunshot boomed.

Screams and shouts filled the air as most civilians ran. A few men fought with soldiers for their rifles.

More shots echoed off the glass and steel.

Three civilians lay dead—sprawled on the curb.

The mob fled.

Soldiers hurried into Humvees and the convoy sped away.

*   *   *

At city hall, six police officers stood outside the lobby keeping several dozen angry and bewildered citizens at bay. While these people were anxious, compared with the hospital and airport, this visit felt like a rest stop. The officers directed Franklin to the Portland Emergency Operations Center, a small room crammed with computers, phones, radios, maps, and whiteboards. Thanks to a generator, lights were on, but nothing else worked. Around a conference table Franklin briefed the mayor, police commissioner, fire chief, and a few others about what he had seen in the city.

The mayor frowned. "That's similar to what we're hearing from the police and fire stations."

"How are you staying in contact with them?" Franklin asked.

"We have a few tow trucks clearing major streets and a few squad cars running," the mayor said. "Can you help us with communications and radios?"

Franklin shook his head. "My orders are to go to Salem and report. Perhaps officials there can provide assistance."

"I hope so." The fire chief frowned.

Franklin returned to the convoy and they rumbled south into the night. Pondering the growing crisis, he realized that most people relied on a complex system to deliver food, water, and medicine.

That system no longer existed.

Day two

Salem, Oregon, Monday, September 5th

Franklin awoke to the screech of metal upon metal grating at his ears. Headlights shined on a tour bus as it tipped over and then slammed into a concrete barrier.

Private Thomas laughed. "Sergeant Keller sure is having fun."

Franklin rubbed his eyes as he stared into the darkness. "Where are we?" His stomach growled as they passed the mangled wreck of the bus.

"Just outside of Salem, sir. There's an MRE on the back seat."

Franklin twisted around, grabbed it, and sighed with relief at the sight of instant coffee inside the package. He slid the packet of coffee into a jacket pocket but, since he hadn't eaten in the last eighteen hours, devoured the rest. Then he pulled out his phone. He had no service, but it did display the time at just past midnight.

Every stop yesterday, eighteen homes, the hospital, airport, city hall, and an electric substation, had proven the same. The power grid remained down and where generators were available, most computer processors were burned out. He held out little hope that the situation would be different in Salem.

The Humvee rumbled onward, swinging past cars and trucks. A fire engine blocked most of the lanes ahead, but Keller swung the deuce around it. Perhaps destroying the bus had satisfied his destructive tendencies for a bit.

Still tired, Franklin considered drinking the coffee, but, wishing to save it for later, he rejected the idea and gradually succumbed to fatigue. He woke to the sound of down-shifting as the convoy slowed to exit the freeway. The sky remained dark with only headlights illuminating the way as they drove toward downtown Salem on streets littered with abandoned vehicles. Tall buildings obscured much of the starry night, as they continued toward the capitol campus.

The deuce ahead slowed and stopped in front of the white marble capitol building, brightened only by lights from within. On either side, light shone from several windows almost as if hung in the sky like stars on a moonless night.

In the distance, an engine, probably a generator, growled.

Franklin stepped from the Humvee onto the pavement. In this open space around the capitol, countless stars dotted the vast night sky. "At least there's no aurora."

Thomas strode around the Humvee and stood beside him. "We had northern lights earlier, sir, while you slept."

Franklin grunted at the news of a second night of solar storms as Sergeant Keller jogged into view. Before he could say anything, two state patrol officers emerged from the darkness and into the glow of the headlights. Each rested a hand on his holster. "Who are you?" one asked.

"I'm Major Franklin. I need to speak with the governor or other command authority."

"First we'll need to see some ID," the officer said flatly.

Franklin pulled the card from his wallet and handed it over.

"I'm Sergeant Benson. The governor and others are still in the emergency command center." Benson examined the card in the glow of the headlights and then returned it. He pulled a flashlight from his belt. "I can take you there."

Turning to Keller, Franklin said, "Have the vehicles refueled and ready to leave when I get back." Then he followed the officer into a nearby gray stone building.

Strategic lights glowed at corners and midway along halls, providing minimal visibility as he and the sergeant moved to the stairwell and headed down. While he had been to the capitol campus many times before and in this building several times, he had never been in the basement. "This is where the emergency center is?"

"Yeah," Benson replied. "It's part of the old bomb shelter complex below the building."

A state patrol officer and a soldier stood guard at the entrance. The soldier asked for ID and then, "Do you have any weapons, sir?"

"Just this." Franklin tapped his holster.

"I'll need it."

Reluctantly, Franklin released it and the guard opened the door.

The stillness of the room struck Franklin. Oregon faced its greatest emergency ever, but the state command center remained as quiet as a library. Only a few hushed voices reached his ears.

A huge map of Oregon covered one wall. Whiteboards filled most of another and several dozen desks covered with computers, phones, and stacks of paper occupied the middle of the room.

He thought of The Cube and how useless it had become since the first CME hit. Perhaps all computers centers were now useless relics of a bygone era. Franklin shook his head, attempting to dismiss the idea and its ultimate consequences.

People turned and stared as Franklin strode across the room. He recognized Governor Adams from his many appearances on television but not the five people with him or the other dozen scattered about.

Adams turned.

"I'm Major Franklin, here on behalf of General Sattler. I've been assessing the situation in Portland and he wanted me to brief you."

Adams nodded and then introduced the state police superintendent, fire marshal, head of emergency management, Salem's mayor, and city police chief. Then the governor sighed. "How bad is it in Portland?"

Franklin described what he had seen the day before.

"So, Portland is in much the same situation as Salem, no power or communication." The governor stared at the floor for a moment. "I hope we'll soon get assistance from the rest of the country or … who knows, maybe Canada can help."

Franklin shook his head. "We suspect most of the world has been hit by the solar storms."

The fire marshal plopped a large binder labeled Emergency Action Plan on a nearby desk. "If that's so, then no one will be able to help us." He frowned and shook his head.

"I believe we need to prepare for that possibility," Franklin replied.

"No," Adams declared. "I won't believe this great nation has been brought down by a storm ... a storm that started millions of miles away on the sun." He shook his head. "It just doesn't make sense."

Franklin knew the facts and those facts did make sense, but he wouldn't argue with the governor. Thinking that it might be a good idea to work with the Oregon National Guard, he asked, "Where's General Gordon?"

"In his office on the second floor." The police superintendent tilted his head as if pointing. "I can show you."

Franklin retrieved his pistol and, with the superintendent, climbed the stairs to an area he had visited several times for meetings and conferences. Just beyond those rooms was a cafeteria. The smell of grease still hung in the air. He had always avoided eating there, but now a burger, fries, and a cup of coffee would have been great. He fingered the pouch of coffee in his pocket.

Later.

Next along the hall stood a small uniform shop used mostly by National Guard soldiers in and around Salem.

Franklin stopped just outside the store. "Do you have the key for this place?"

"I have a master key." The superintendent raised an eyebrow. "You need to get in there?"

"Yes."

The superintendent shrugged, unlocked the door, and held it open.

Inside, Franklin searched a dozen drawers behind the counter until he spotted what he needed. Stuffing the necessary items in a pocket, he set a ten-dollar bill by the register as he left.

Just around the next corner the superintendent stopped at General Gordon's office.

The superintendent introduced Franklin to the general, a man with thinning gray hair and a wrinkled brow.

"What can I do for you, Major? Or what can we do for each other?"

The superintendent left, and for the next few minutes Franklin and Gordon discussed ideas for working together to provide security.

Static crackled from a corner of the room.

Franklin turned and spotted a small multiband transceiver. "It's good to see you have one that works."

"I had it in a Faraday cage the night of the storms and took it out only today." Gordon adjusted the squelch.

"You know about Faraday cages?" Franklin smiled.

"They say you can't teach an old dog new tricks." He flashed a broad grin. "I read the military journals and try to keep up."

Franklin laughed.

"We had auroras earlier." Gordon shrugged. "It still works. I think I heard your drivers talking as you entered Salem. I tried to contact them, but the signal isn't good in this building."

They returned to their security discussion until Franklin said, "I think we have a framework, but I'll need to return to Portland before—"

Keller burst into the room with a police officer behind him. Gasping, he said, "There's a guard unit under attack ... just outside of Salem. We heard them ... over the radio."

"Where?" Franklin stood.

Keller took a deep breath. "At an armory just east of here, sir."

Franklin looked at General Gordon. The martial law decree made him the senior officer in the state.

"I know this isn't your mission, Major," General Gordon frowned. "But I have no troops with me."

"Sergeant Keller, have the soldiers do buddy checks and then perform the pre-combat inspection."

"Yes, sir." He hurried from the room.

"I know the place." General Gordon retrieved a pistol and holster from his desk and stood. "I'm going with you."

The general grabbed his radio and followed Franklin. When they stepped outside, the radio crackled to life. "...attackers ... main building ... wearing ACUs."

The men stood in formation when Franklin arrived at the vehicles.

Sergeant Keller saluted. "Buddy checks and PCI completed. The platoon is ready, but ah, sir, what about Katie and my boy?"

With all that had happened, Franklin had forgotten them. "They'll need to stay here. We'll come back and pick them up."

Franklin moved to the front of the formation and stared at the young faces. Tonight they would go into battle, but most of his twenty soldiers were young and untested. Nearly a third of them were computer specialists, nerds, not infantry. Sure, they had fired on people at the airport but out of fear, not on orders. This time they would need to fire with the intent to kill. Franklin tried to find just the right tone, serious but not worried or scared. "Traitors, wearing army uniforms, have attacked and probably killed fellow soldiers. We need to stop them. We may need to kill them. When I give the order, you will shoot to kill these traitors. Any questions?" His gaze moved along the line of wide-eyed and frightened young faces. "Okay then, tonight we earn our stripes."

"Hooah," the soldiers shouted.

"Mount up," Franklin ordered.

General Gordon followed Franklin to his Humvee. As they climbed in, Franklin looked to the back seat and asked, "What's the quickest way there?"

Gordon thrust an arm forward. "Go straight ahead to the next intersection and turn left."

Franklin relayed the information over the radio to Keller.

As the convoy sped down the road, the radio erupted into static that then gave way to a frightened voice. "Any station … guard unit at … Anderson … under fire … forty or fifty … unknown … Any station …"

The voice faded and the static ceased. Franklin turned to Gordon. "How many people do you have at armory?"

"A twelve-man squad."

Franklin grabbed the mic as a dozen ideas fought for attention. The enemy might also have a radio. What could he say? What could he ask? What was the forty or fifty reference? Would they be going into this fight outnumbered? He decided to keep it simple and pressed transmit. "Anderson armory, this is army convoy. Maintain position. We're en route to your location."

"Roger … attackers are in the main building."

Thomas turned down the next street. "Are these guys soldiers? Why would they attack an armory?"

"Probably a militia group," Gordon said from the back seat. "There are everything from M4s to rocket launchers and night-vision gear at that armory. They may see this as a good time to take it."

"Army convoy," the scared voice again sounded over the radio. "I'm on the roof with one other soldier. Five others have retreated to the arms room. I don't know the location of the others but believe they are combat-ineffective."

"Whoever they are, they're now our enemy," Gordon cursed. "Major, we need to eliminate them before they kill more soldiers or civilians."

"Yes, sir."

Gordon leaned forward. "The armory is less than a mile ahead."

The sound of gunfire echoed among the buildings.

"Convoy, lights off," Franklin ordered over the radio. "The vehicles crept forward in near total darkness. He hoped the clamor of battle concealed the noise of their engines.

Gordon pointed ahead. "There! On the left. Muzzle flashes."

The convoy pulled to the side of the road and squads hurried through the darkness toward the fury of combat. Four men positioned behind cars fired at two soldiers on the roof of the gray three-story stone building.

Using binoculars, Franklin located the men in the parking lot. They did wear ACUs, but two didn't have helmets and one wore what looked like a German pickelhaube. "Anderson Armory, hold your fire on targets outside. We're coming in." Franklin pulled the pistol from his holster and ordered his men to fire on those in the parking lot, and then took the first shot.

On either side of Franklin came the bang of gunfire in quick three-round bursts that left the four attackers sprawled on the pavement.

Franklin ran to the four where blood and trauma confirmed all were dead. He grabbed an AR-15 from one of the bodies and borrowed a magazine from one of his men.

A young soldier slumped to a knee and puked.

Franklin waved the others forward and all hurried across the parking lot toward the main entrance. Nearing the glass doors, he spotted a young man apparently left behind to guard the entrance.

The boy lifted his rifle.

Franklin fired first, shattering the glass of one door. Another shot followed from Keller and both hit the boy in the chest. The kid dropped with an audible thud.

Inside the lobby, Franklin tried not to stare. He had killed a child not much older than his son.

Bursts of gunfire continued from somewhere in the building.

"The arms room is in the basement." Gordon gestured down a dark hall. "This way."

Franklin clicked transmit. "Anderson Armory, we are in the building and proceeding to the arms room."

Shots tore through the blackness. General Gordon stumbled backward and fell to the floor.

Keller returned fire down the hall.

Franklin joined him, firing at the muzzle flashes as others joined the fight.

*   *   *

The tiny battery-powered lamp cast dark shadows across the armory commander's office where Franklin sat alone. Using a hot pack, he warmed the coffee he had saved from the MRE. Only minutes ago they had captured the last terrorist in the building when he ran out of ammo. How many had escaped from the building? Where did they go? Perhaps the prisoner could provide answers.

He leaned back in the chair and struggled to remember details and the sequence of events that occurred during the night. Exhaustion rolled over him like waves on a beach, but he needed to write his report. Good soldiers had died, including General Gordon. There would be an investigation. Where was Keller? He needed the list of dead and wounded.

The events of the night seemed foggy and disjointed. His soldiers, along with the remnants of the armory squad, had secured the building. That was clear, but exactly how they had achieved it faded from his mind like a dream. No, a nightmare.

Bile rose in his throat, but he resisted the urge to puke.

Keller entered and saluted. "Here's the list. General Gordon is dead, along with four others from the armory squad, one is wounded, and two are missing. From our platoon we have three dead, Burns, Allen, and Garcia."

"I thought Garcia was wounded."

"He *was*." Keller frowned. "Now we have two wounded, Thomas and Palmer, but Corporal Bickel thinks they'll be okay."

Franklin pointed to a bloodstain low on Keller's right leg. "Are you wounded?"

"Oh." The sergeant pulled on a rip in his uniform. "I guess so." He winced and cursed as he examined it. "Looks like a graze. It'll be fine, but it really stings now that I see it."

One of the soldiers from the armory squad darted into the office. Franklin struggled to recall his name, Hanford ... no, Hansen, Corporal Hansen.

"Excuse me, sir. We found Private Clark, one of the missing soldiers; his body was in a nearby alley." He paused and bit his lip. "The militia ... they slit his throat."

Anger flared in Franklin. "What about the other missing soldier?"

"She's still missing?"

"She?"

"Yes, sir. Private Jessica Davis."

Franklin imagined his wife, Carol, captured by these thugs and anger burned within him. "Bring the man we captured here. I want to talk with him."

The two returned with the prisoner, wearing a frayed and faded army uniform.

"You don't deserve to wear that uniform. Take it off," Franklin ordered.

The man cursed. "Try and take it off me!"

Franklin smiled. "You heard the prisoner."

Keller and Hansen threw the prisoner to the floor. He wrestled with the two soldiers until Franklin walked around the desk and pressed a gun to his head.

Moments later, wearing only socks, T-shirt and underwear, Keller and Hansen zip-tied the man's wrists to the chair.

"He had an AR-15 modified for full automatic," Keller said as he worked. "That's probably why he ran out of ammo. He also had this." He pulled a combat knife from his pocket and passed it to Franklin. "Should we stay while you interrogate him?"

Franklin nodded as he examined the knife. Without looking up, he asked, "What's your name?"

The man spat on the floor. "I want a lawyer."

Okay stupid, if that's the way you want to do this. "Where did your friends take Private Davis?"

"*Lawyer,*" he said slowly.

"Sure, what's their phone number?" Franklin held the phone receiver to his ear and then faked a frown and disappointment. "Sorry, no dial tone."

Keller chuckled.

"You should just let me go. It won't be long before guys like you are swept aside. We're going to be part of the Sovereign Militia, and we're going to rule in the days ahead. You're part of the weak and decaying old system. We are the power and the future."

Stupid was right. The storms had swept away the old order. A new society would rise out of the present chaos, but right now force ruled. He stared at Stupid. This terrorist and his cohort wanted to rule by force and they could.

The only thing necessary for the triumph of evil is for good men to do nothing. The quote from Edmund Burke rolled around in Franklin's mind along with worries about his own wife and family. He needed to find Davis, eliminate this militia group, and return home with his men as quickly as possible. He didn't know exactly how, but he would get the information he needed from this man by any means necessary.

Any means necessary. What did that mean? How far could he go? He decided to leave the philosophical questions for later as an idea formed in his mind.

Franklin pushed the cup of coffee forward. "I just made it. Would you like some? Perhaps we can come to an understanding."

"Now you're talking." Stupid grinned and looked down at his wrists.

"Release his left arm," Franklin ordered.

When free, Stupid reached for the coffee.

Franklin slammed the knife through his hand, pinning it to the table and spilling the coffee.

Keller's eyes flared open and Hansen's mouth hung agape.

Stupid screamed and cursed. "Take it out! Are you crazy?"

"Maybe. Do I have your attention now?"

Stupid stared as blood flowed from his hand, mixing with the coffee. With ashen face, he nodded.

"Good." Franklin rested his hand on the butt of the knife. "What's your name?"

Stupid's gaze darted from his hand to Franklin. "Huh?"

"Your name?" Franklin wiggled the knife.

"Uh, Rick."

"Good start." Using one finger, Franklin jiggled the knife. "Your full name."

"Rick." He grimaced and cursed. "Richard Dean Harlan."

Franklin grinned. "Okay, Dick. Do you mind if I call you Dick?"

He shook his head.

"Where did your friends take Private Davis?"

Day three

Salem, Oregon, Tuesday, September 6th

As the gray light of a cloudy dawn filtered through an office window, Franklin believed he had extracted all the information Dick Harlan could provide.

All of the blood and death had been on his own authority and those decisions might mean prison or at least the end of his career. Still, Franklin felt he had done the right thing. If he hadn't come to the aid of the armory squad, all of them would have been killed or captured and the weapons taken, making the militia group an even greater threat.

Even interrogation of Dick … no torture … that's what it was … what the charge would be at his court-martial … even that brutal act seemed to have been the right choice. After some initial reluctance, Dick had eagerly answered every question.

Franklin wiped the bloody knife on the prisoner's T-shirt. "How old is Private Davis?" he asked Corporal Hansen.

"Eighteen. She graduated from high school in June."

Franklin thought of his son. This would be his senior year of high school, if the school opened. For a moment he imagined his own son as an army private in this collapsing world. He shuddered.

"I had nothing to do with kidnapping that girl or killing that other guy you found." Now with both arms free, Dick cradled his bloody hand against his T-shirt. "I need a doctor."

Franklin stared at him for a moment. "You'll get one—when we get Private Davis back." As he continued to glare at Dick, Franklin could almost see the slow cogs of the man's brain working. What would happen to him if they didn't get Davis back? Franklin decided to answer that question. "If you've lied to us or left something out, I'll let that hand rot. But if you've been honest and complete in your answers, we'll take care of you."

"I told you everything I know. All of it." Dick nodded vigorously.

Franklin believed him. "Handcuff Dickey in one of the trucks heading south with us," he ordered Keller and Parson. "And have the medic bandage his hand."

Moments later, alone in the office, Franklin finished his report, signed it, and sealed the pages in an envelope. His fate and that of the prisoner rested with General Sattler. Bulging envelope in hand, he walked to the parking lot.

Franklin stepped outside just as Keller finished the pre-combat inspection. "The platoon is ready, sir. I added the armory soldiers in with two of our squads."

"Form up the men," Franklin said. "I'll speak with them in a moment." He continued on to the deuce that would transport the wounded back to Portland.

Thomas leaned out the passenger window and saluted. "Ready to leave when you say so, sir."

"I thought you were wounded." Franklin raised an eyebrow. "What're you doing sitting up here?"

"I can't walk, but I can shoot if it's needed."

Franklin nodded and handed him the envelope with the after-action report. "Pick up Keller's wife and child. Then don't stop for anything on your way back to Portland. When you arrive, take this report directly to General Sattler."

"Yes, sir."

The truck rolled from the parking lot and down the street. The moment it disappeared, Franklin thought of his family. He hadn't been gone long but should have included a letter to them. He should have allowed all the soldiers an opportunity to send notes home. Cursing his slow thinking, Franklin walked back toward the remaining soldiers and vehicles.

"Attention!" Sergeant Keller ordered.

Looking over the soldiers that he would lead on the rescue mission, Franklin marveled at their youth. Some were barely out of high school, but, in the last couple of days, all of them had seen combat. He didn't see fear in their eyes, only anger, and determination. They were few, less than forty in number, but they were ready. "Soldiers, we are not going to leave Private Davis or anyone else behind. Let's go find her, bring her back, and deal with those who took her."

"Hooah," the soldiers shouted back.

Pride surged within Franklin. They were young, but they were soldiers. "Mount up!"

*   *   *

Franklin and the rest of the convoy rolled south out of Salem along the route Dick had said the militia traveled on their way up to Salem. Dick said they had used trees, shrubs, and gullies along the roadside to hide much of their movement and would likely use the same as they traveled back to their compound.

Picking up speed, the convoy soon rolled through the small town of Turner and continued south toward Jefferson along a two-lane highway through the farms and fields of the Willamette Valley. A beautiful setting, but Franklin focused his gaze like a hawk in search of prey. The fields, vines, and fruit trees were of no interest to him today; he sought one thing, the militia that had attacked and killed his comrades. As they drove south, Franklin continued to scan the surroundings that soon changed from farms to a large forest of evergreen trees.

The radio crackled with Keller's voice. "Gunfire and smoke ahead."

"Convoy, stop! Deploy as planned," Franklin ordered. With binoculars in hand, he exited the Humvee and hunched low in the gully beside the road. He hoped the noise and confusion of combat hid his approach, and that of the rest of his soldiers, as they moved toward a bend in the road.

Two squads followed Franklin on the right side of the pavement. On the left, the other two squads hurried forward with Keller.

Ahead, men shouted, gunfire boomed, and bullets pinged as Franklin crawled into position to observe the battle. A convoy of two police vehicles and six pickups and vans were pinned down along the curve in the highway by a group firing from a blockade of abandoned vehicles and from a roadside knoll.

Over the radio, Franklin explained the situation to Keller. "My two squads will attack the hill. You flank the group on the road and attack the opposite side."

The moment his men were in attack position, Franklin shouted, "Fire!"

A thunderous cacophony of gunfire erupted.

At that moment, Franklin spotted a female soldier leaning against a rock near the crest of the knoll. Gagged and handcuffed, she struggled to stay low and move away.

The militia on the knoll continued to return fire but then, in a flurry of activity, scurried back toward the forest, like animals returning to the safety of their lair. One militiaman grabbed the woman by the hair, pulled her up, and shoved her forward.

Franklin pointed toward the edge of the forest. "Cut them off. They have Davis!" Soldiers ran toward the tree line as Franklin gave orders for Keller to flank the militia from the other side, and then followed his soldiers into the woods.

Rifle fire thundered among the trees.

Franklin aimed at the man holding Davis but never had a clear shot.

Then the enemy, along with Davis, disappeared amid the trees and shrubs.

"Hold your fire," Franklin shouted. Then he stared into the forest and whispered, "You won't get away. We know where you're going."

As he left the forest near the site of the ambush, Franklin cursed. Four nervous police officers pointed guns at him from behind a truck and two squad cars. The men ranged from young to an older man with wrinkled skin, bulky frame, and salt-and-pepper hair. Another six civilians, both men and women inched out of hiding. Two had rifles, the others didn't.

"Stop!" Salt and Pepper ordered. "Drop your weapons."

Keller and the two squads with him jogged along the highway toward the nervous group.

Franklin held up his hand, signaling Keller to stop. Then Franklin said to Salt and Pepper, "We're the good guys. We're after that militia group."

"How can I be sure?"

Franklin gazed at his soldiers in a semicircle surrounding most of the civilians and police. "Well, if we were the militia that attacked you, I think you'd all be dead by now."

Salt and Pepper followed Franklin's gaze. "Your point is taken." He eased his weapon lower. "I'm Lieutenant Crowley with the Linn County Sheriff's Office. My officer friends here are with the Lebanon City Police. We were bringing food and water for our families and neighbors when they attacked."

Franklin passed his rifle to another soldier and walked down the knoll. Standing near Crowley, he slowly pulled out his ID and passed it to the officer.

Crowley looked it over, passed it back, and then they shook hands.

"The militia is heading south." Franklin pulled out a map and pointed to the area. "If you're going in this general direction, we can escort you."

"Yes." Crowley's eyes narrowed as he studied the chart. "We're headed back to a neighborhood in south Lebanon."

Engine oil and coolant linked from both police cars and bullets had flattened three tires of one van. After moving supplies to the other trucks, the remaining vehicles took position at the end of the convoy as it continued south. Minutes later, just outside of town, a group of men, women, and children waved frantically at the convoy.

Franklin ordered the vehicles to stop. "Soldiers, deploy with your weapons."

Hansen stopped the Humvee. "They don't look dangerous."

"After all we've been through, I'm not taking the chance." Franklin stepped from the vehicle.

"People with guns tried to kill us," a man in his thirties shouted and gestured to Keller, still in his vehicle. A dozen men, women, and children stood nearby.

Franklin strode toward the group. "Where were you attacked?"

One woman stood close beside the man as he pointed toward Lebanon. "It was in a park in town."

"Show me." Franklin unfolded his map.

The man pointed. "This is where it happened."

"What else can you tell me?"

"Not much really. I was asleep and all of a sudden there was a lot of shooting and screaming. I grabbed my wife and kids and ran. All of us did."

Others nodded agreement.

"But ... there was a neighbor boy with us," the woman said and then paused for a long moment. "We can't find him."

"We're headed that way." Franklin folded his map. Could the militia be the attackers in the park? He shook his head. The group they were following would still be en route to Lebanon. Whoever attacked here had been in town before dawn. "We'll see what we can find out." But he didn't want to delay long. They needed to free Davis and neutralize the militia group. Since they had left Salem, a plan had formed in his mind, but they needed to get ahead of these thugs. They needed to keep moving. "Mount up!"

The convoy continued its trek into town, but before the park, Franklin ordered them to stop. From there he deployed the men in two groups to flank any shooters still in the area.

Minutes later, from the woods just outside the park, Franklin looked through binoculars. One man, carrying a shotgun and with a dog on a leash, walked casually from body to body while a brunette-haired woman screamed and cried nearby. He pressed transmit. "Does anyone have eyes on a threat?"

"Negative," a corporal responded over the radio.

The speaker crackled again. "Just a crying woman, a guy with a dog, and several bodies."

Franklin nodded and pressed transmit. "Drivers, pull your vehicles forward. Squads, keep watch on the perimeter. I'll handle the man." He signaled for Hansen and Braun to advance with him. As they cleared the woods, he shouted, "Halt! Put your hands up!"

The trucks rumbled into view.

The man turned as if to run but then stopped and raised his hands.

The dog barked wildly and Hansen aimed his rifle at the animal.

Franklin didn't want any shooting at man or beast, but before he could say anything to the soldier, the civilian lowered his arm. Franklin tensed and gripped his pistol.

"No!" The muscles in his neck and jaw tensed as he pulled the dog close. "We haven't done anything wrong."

"Hand over the shotgun and tie the dog to the tree," Franklin ordered.

The civilian handed the gun to Braun and tied the animal to a nearby tree. Braun frisked the man and pulled a pistol from his jacket.

"Aren't you well-armed?" Franklin asked sarcastically as he examined the well-oiled Sig P250 pistol. "Did you kill these people?"

"No!" The man shook his head. "Of course not. I'm just trying to get home, Major."

"Sure looked like you were trying to get away." Franklin waved his hand. "Come with us."

The civilian fixed his gaze on the officer. "Am I under arrest?"

"No." Franklin gritted his teeth. He didn't want to waste time arguing so he stepped close and, in his most authoritative voice, said, "But the state is under martial law so not doing what I say could get you arrested—or shot."

"What about my dog?"

"I guess freedom for both of you depends upon your answers," Franklin said flatly. "Were you in the service?"

"Yes. Four years enlisted in the navy." The man glanced back at the dog. "How did you know?"

"You got my rank right."

As they walked away, the dog whimpered.

Two soldiers from the armory group led the hysterical woman back toward the convoy.

"No!" She shouted and struggled with the men, then pushed one and bit the other on the arm.

The soldiers threw her to the ground with a thud, yanked her wrists to her back, and zip-tied them. Then they pulled her upright. Blood flowed from her nose and lips.

Franklin stared at the giggling woman and then the soldiers. Two days of combat had left him suspicious and edgy. All these young soldiers were tense and the woman might be crazy. Franklin looked at the man they had just taken into custody. His eyes were wide with fear.

"What do you need to know?" the man asked.

Franklin ignored the question and, as they neared the convoy, turned to a private. "If he tries to escape, stop him but try not to kill him. I want answers."

"Yes, sir."

The private looked more like a boy with his first gun than a combat veteran. Franklin nodded and walked away. He wasn't too worried about the young soldier shooting an unarmed man. He had meant the "try not to kill him" comment as a caution to the prisoner to stay put.

Ten yards away, Franklin approached Crowley and another police officer. "I think whoever launched this attack has moved on."

Crowley glared at the prisoner. "Is he one of the attackers?"

"I don't think so, but I'll talk with him before we continue south."

With a deep breath, Crowley seemed to let the anger flow out of him. "Our families are probably worried about us. We'll be heading home."

They shook hands and then the police and civilians departed.

Franklin spread his map on the tailgate of one of the trucks and, with an elbow on one end and a hand on the other, bent over to hold the paper down against the breeze while he studied it. Thanks to Dick, they knew the location of the militia compound. If the militia remained on foot, Franklin felt confident that his soldiers would stay ahead of them. The group that attacked this park seemed much more professional than the group they fought last night and this morning. Franklin let out a low groan at the thought of fighting two militias.

After several more moments of study, he stood straight and rubbed his back. Sleeping in a Humvee had left him tired and sore.

"Could you use a table and chair?" Keller and Private Braun offered up a camp table and several folding chairs. "We found these."

"That'll make this much easier." Franklin pointed to a group of nearby trees. "Set them up over there." He sat at the table and looked again at the map but soon turned away with a sigh. He needed more information. Addressing Braun, still nearby, he called, "Private, bring the prisoner and his belongings to me."

"Yes, sir."

Franklin folded his map and anchored it to the table with a stone. He would start the interview the same way he had with Dick. Franklin didn't think this new man was involved in the attack here, but the man's willingness to talk and the answers he provided would guide the questioning.

Braun and another soldier escorted the prisoner to where Franklin sat. The private held out his hand. "Sir, the prisoner had this small knife in the bag but no other weapons or suspicious items."

Franklin took the knife, examined it, and set it on the table. He hoped the blade wouldn't be needed. "My name is Major Franklin." He gestured for the man to sit in one of the empty chairs.

"Neal." The chair rocked on the uneven ground. "Uh, Neal Evans."

Franklin gave a slow nod and allowed a slight smile. This interview was already off to a better start. "Since the solar storm, we've had problems with looters and the general criminal element. We've had a particularly bad time with one militia group that has been raiding and killing in this area."

"I have nothing to do with them or what happened here."

"I don't think you do either, but somehow everyone else in that park ended up dead or crazy." He leaned forward. "So, tell me what happened. Who was in the park when you arrived?"

"Thirty, maybe forty, men, women, and children."

"Were they armed?" Franklin wrote the numbers on a yellow legal pad. "Did there appear to be any military organization?"

"No. They seemed like a bunch of refugees."

Franklin made notes for his next report. "Go on."

"Later, eight men came into the meadow. They looked like a biker gang, minus the bikes. I thought they might be a problem."

"Where were you when they arrived?"

"In the trees just to the west." Neal pointed to where he had camped. "Anyway, after a while things settled down, and I fell asleep. Just before dawn, rapid gunfire erupted. I stayed low until there was enough light to see."

"So, all the shooting happened while it was still dark?"

Neal nodded. "I think they must have had night-vision gear. They killed the bikers in seconds. I think the other bodies in the meadow were collateral damage."

Calling the dead civilians collateral damage surprised Franklin, even if it was an accurate description. Had the world changed so much in three days? Apparently. Franklin jotted more notes for his report.

"Please, you've got to believe me. I'm just trying to get home. I didn't kill anyone."

"I believe you." Franklin slid the knife back to Neal. It seemed probable he was telling the truth and so Franklin decided to release him, but use Dick as a final test. "Will you be going through Portland?"

"You're letting me go?"

Franklin nodded.

"Yeah, I'll need to go through parts of the city." A smile grew on Neal's face. "I'll probably avoid the downtown area. Can you tell me what the situation is in Portland now?"

Franklin shook his head. "I wish I knew. My family lives there." For the next couple of minutes, he wrote. Then he sealed each of two pages in its own envelope and wrote on the covers. Holding one up, he said, "This is for my commanding officer in Portland. If you make it there, I've asked him to provide you safe passage through the city."

"Thank you. Who is the other letter for?"

"My wife and children. Please let them know that I'm okay."

When Neal walked out of hearing range, Franklin sent for Keller. "Take a couple of soldiers and walk Dick past Neal as he's leaving. Mention Dick's real name, Richard Harlin, as you go by and keep a close eye on both of them. If either reacts, arrest Neal."

"We gave Neal his weapons back."

Franklin nodded. "Hopefully Neal and Dickey don't know each other, but if either does react, arrest Neal if you can, kill him if you must."

Day four

Linn County, Oregon, Wednesday, September 7th

Franklin stood by the trucks watching as his soldiers rained bullets on the civilians in the meadow.

No!

Dick stood in the center of the clearing with his bloody hand held high above his head. As the rounds hit closer Neal wandered in the meadow. He walked by and Dick smiled at him.

Gunfire mowed them both down.

No!

He thought the words, but he couldn't say them.

The crazy woman laughed as she strolled aimlessly among the dead. Guns thundered and she fell giggling and bleeding to the ground.

No! He tried to shout the command, but it remained just a thought, leaving him a mute witness as the carnage continued.

General Gordon and Private Davis sprinted out of the forest. Muzzle flashes lit the night and they fell in bloody heaps.

Next, Franklin's son, James, ran out of the trees on the far side of the meadow. His son sped ever closer, dodging bullets that pinged and ricocheted around him.

Franklin reached out his hand and then a single round struck James in the chest and he fell.

Thud.

Franklin bolted awake.

"Sorry for the bump, sir." Corporal Hansen downshifted. "We turned on to the side road. The ambush position is about a mile ahead."

"Thank you, Corporal." A dream. It had all been a dream. No, another nightmare. Franklin took a deep breath, rubbed his face and eyes.

Most of the people Franklin recognized in the dream: his son, Neal, even the crazy woman, and Dick, were probably fine, or as fine as they could be. Unfortunately, the only people he could check on right now were Dick and the woman. Keller had reported that Dick had been complaining about his hand when he passed near Neal, but neither gave any notice of the other. Dick was probably still whining in one of the trucks behind him and the woman was probably giggling or crying.

But what about Neal? Franklin hoped that Neal would soon reach Portland, deliver the messages, and head on home.

"Fork in the road." Keller's voice came over the radio.

"Convoy, halt," Franklin ordered. "Soldiers, deploy with weapons." The ambush would take place just over the next hill.

Hansen stopped the Humvee and Franklin pushed the nightmare from his mind as he exited. The trucks pulled up one fork of the road into the darkness as the soldiers formed up along the pavement edge of the other road.

"Get the squad leaders and meet me on the top of that hill," Franklin pointed and then strode across the road and into the forest. Reaching the crest of the knoll, he scanned the valley below in the dim light of a crescent moon. The area appeared much as he had envisioned from his map. The road curved around the hill and then dropped into a narrow river valley. A two-lane bridge provided the only dry way across the water.

A twig snapped behind him and Franklin turned to see a dark figure moving toward him. He rested his hand on his holster.

"It's me, sir, Keller. The squad leaders are coming. I thought I'd keep watch while you planned."

"I'm pretty much done with planning." But Franklin continued to study the surrounding terrain for a moment and then pulled his map and two hand-drawn diagrams from a pocket as the final element of his plan took shape.

When everyone had arrived, Franklin gathered them near as he pointed to the valley. "This is where we fight. Keller, take three squads to the other side and get cover and camouflage along both sides of the road. Then, when *all* of the militia thugs are on the west side of the river, I'll give the command to open fire."

Keller pointed to the bridge. "They'll want to retreat back across it."

"They'll be very exposed if they do," Franklin said. "I'll remain on this side with one squad and block the bridge. I'll radio for the Humvees to rush up and provide additional cover."

"What about Private Davis?" Corporal Hansen asked in a worried tone. "We're going to be shooting in her direction."

"I hope the militia arrives after dawn so we can spot her more easily or that they surrender quickly." Franklin bit his lip. Neither seemed likely. "She's a soldier. She'll need to help us help her."

Hansen still looked worried, and Franklin wasn't happy with his answer so decided to change the subject. He pointed to a diagram of the militia compound. "Dickey says that only the women were left to guard the place. Apparently, these candidates for the Sovereign Militia are very patriarchal. After we're done here, we'll confirm that."

"Who drew the map, sir?" Keller asked.

"Dick," Franklin said. "Good thing I didn't stab his writing hand."

"Do you trust him?"

"Of course not, but I'm certain that he doesn't want me mad either. Does everyone understand the plan?"

"Yes, sir." Keller looked at the battle map and then gestured across the river. "You want me and three of the squads under cover just inside the forest on the west bank."

"Yes." Franklin folded his maps. "We have only enough night-vision gear for me, the senior NCO, and the squad leaders. Make sure you get a set and deploy with your squads."

"Hooah," the squad leaders replied and then left to prepare for battle.

*   *   *

Despite inspecting every position and reviewing the battle plan with each squad, Franklin remained unsettled. His mouth felt dry and his stomach churned so loud he thought the soldiers might hear it. If the militia arrived before dawn, then Franklin and his soldiers would have the tactical advantage. However, the chance of shooting Davis would be higher. As he crossed the bridge back to the east bank, static erupted from his radio.

"This is lookout one." Franklin recognized the voice of Private Joe Rankin, a red-haired kid who might have been nineteen. "A group of … ah … twenty, no twenty-five individuals approaching my position on the road below."

"Roger. Advise when they have passed." Franklin's stomach twisted. This must be the militia. He looked into a sky still filled with stars.

Moments later, the radio crackled again. "This is lookout one. The group has passed. Too dark to see Davis."

"Roger. Proceed to your next position."

Franklin raced up the knoll. Even before he had reached the spot where his soldiers watched and waited, he could hear the people coming. Images from his dream raced through his mind. He didn't want gunfire raining down on innocent civilians.

Thumps of boots on pavement warned of their arrival.

Franklin hunkered down with his soldiers and struggled to get the night-vision gear on. He needed to make sure this was the militia group and not just a bunch of refugees returning home. As the night morphed into a green monochrome view, he scanned for Davis.

The group converged to cross the bridge.

Franklin whispered into the radio. "Hold your fire until I can ident—"

A gunshot boomed, followed by a moment of silence. Then the night filled with the sound of gunfire. Men screamed and fell to the ground and into the water.

"Cease-fire!" Franklin shouted to those nearby and over the radio. "Cease-fire!" Had his dream come true? Had they fired on a bunch of civilian refugees? He didn't know.

The Humvees raced into position, blocking retreat, but didn't open fire.

As the gunfire waned, two people jumped to their feet on the bridge. They struggled for a moment then, with hands close together, the smaller hit the larger person in the groin.

Davis?

A flash of shoulder-length hair confirmed his thought. He couldn't tell the color of her hair, but the length seemed right for the woman he had spotted earlier in the day.

Davis hit the man in the chest, spun around, and jumped into the water with a loud splash.

Franklin pressed transmit. "Open fire; that's Davis in the water."

A few thugs scattered along the west bank and fell in seconds. A dozen more hunkered low on the bridge while most scurried back the way they had come.

"Fire!" Franklin pointed at the retreating militia. "Humvees advance."

Guns thundered and engines roared.

Within a minute, everyone on or near the bridge was dead or wounded. A lone figure ran across the battlefield and dove into the water. Moments later, two struggled up the riverbank.

Four thugs held up their hands near the bridge. "Stop! Don't shoot," one of them shouted.

Franklin stood. "Cease-fire."

Moans and cries of pain greeted the dawn.

*   *   *

After the battle, as Franklin walked among the soldiers, he noticed Corporal Hansen and Private Davis sitting nearby with blankets wrapped about them. The two talked to each other and smiled as they shivered. One of the soldiers brought them coffee. Where did they get coffee?

As the battle had waned, Hansen had left his position, and his squad, run to Davis, and pulled her from the water. That action, and the looks and smiles they now shared, told Franklin all he needed to know. He walked over and the two jumped to their feet.

"How are you doing, Private Davis?"

"Well, sir …." A slight grin formed. "I'm just glad to be free."

"Did the medic check you over?"

"Not yet, sir. She's been busy with the wounded. I'm okay. They were in such a hurry to get back to their compound, they didn't have time to do much more than knock me about a bit."

"I'm glad you weren't seriously hurt." He turned and walked away. The issue of their romance and Hansen's actions during the battle could wait for another day.

Franklin climbed the hillside and sat near where he had led the battle. He should have felt pleased; none of his men had died. Three were wounded, but they would live, show off their scars, and tell stories about the day. He swallowed a long slow drink of water. Below, on the dry grass near the bridge, Bickel, the medic, struggled to save one wounded militia member. Nearby Private Michael Kohen held an IV bag over another wounded thug.

The battle hadn't gone as planned. Did they ever? But at least it had been lopsided in their favor. Franklin pulled a notepad from his pocket. General Sattler would want a report. Of the twenty-two militiamen who had reached this point, fourteen were dead. The two receiving medical attention might soon boost that number.

Keller jogged up the hill and saluted. "Sir, the recon team returned. It looks like Dick told the truth. The team watched the compound for several hours and spotted only a handful of women."

Franklin nodded. "We'll leave them be and head for home."

"What about the dead?" Keller looked down by the river where bodies had been laid in two side-by-side rows. "We don't have many shovels, but it seems wrong to just leave them there."

"Have the men gather dry wood."

"Huh, ah, sir?"

"Do you know what a funeral pyre is?"

Hours later, the fire roared and the smell of burnt flesh mixed with smoke as the convoy rumbled away, leaving the dead behind.

Day five

Salem, Oregon, Thursday, September 8th

When convoy headlights illuminated a "Welcome to Salem" sign, anxiousness grew in Franklin. This would be a quick stop. Just brief Governor Adams, turn over the crazy woman, Dick, and the other prisoners, and then head for home. He imagined greeting his wife and sons, eating the customary welcome-home breakfast of eggs, toast, bacon, and coffee, and snatching a few hours of sleep in his own bed. Those were simple pleasures, but they were all he needed.

He sighed. Even if breakfast consisted of only cold cereal or an MRE, he would at least eat it at home.

Hoping to check the time, he pulled his phone from a pocket. The device showed a low battery and shut off. He had a charger with him, but the Humvee had no place to plug it in. Perhaps he could recharge the phone at the Cyber Intel Center, but what if he couldn't? He had taken dozens of pictures on the recent camping trip with James. Would he ever be able to share them with Carol?

"Capitol building ahead, sir," Keller radioed from the lead vehicle.

Before Franklin could reply, a bright light swept across the Humvee.

"Two spotlights." Keller's terse voice emanated from the radio. "Some sort of barricade ahead."

"Convoy, stop," Franklin ordered over the radio. He thought about having the vehicles shut off their headlights and then retreat, but they were on the edge of the capitol campus. This must be a police roadblock. He pressed transmit. "Keller, can you see anything?"

"Just bright lights and black beyond, sir."

"Roger." Franklin eased from the Humvee and walked toward Keller's deuce.

Several lights shifted onto him.

"Identify yourselves," someone shouted.

The voice sounded familiar. "Major Franklin, with the army convoy from Portland. We were here ...uh." He thought for a second. It seemed so long ago. "We were here on Monday." More lights focused on him.

"Major Franklin, advance and be identified."

As Franklin stepped forward, a sandbagged roadblock emerged from the gloom. Several armed men were now visible. "Continue forward," the familiar voice ordered.

Franklin did, and gradually faces came into better view. One of the men smiled. "Welcome back, Major Franklin."

"Hello again, Sergeant Benson."

The police officer smiled and turned to those beside him. "Let the trucks in."

As the vehicles rolled by, Franklin spoke with Benson. "I need to brief the governor and others. Also, we have seven militia prisoners."

"Do you need food, fuel, or ammo?"

"Hot food, if you've got any."

"I'll take care of your soldiers." Benson turned to another police officer. "Take Major Franklin to the colonel."

Following the police officer, Franklin crossed the wide plaza. Along the grassy edges, several wooden poles had been erected with lights hanging from them, creating a streetlight glow. But Benson led him into the shadows toward the dark building where he had met with General Gordon and other leaders three days earlier. Inside, they climbed upstairs, past the now-open cafeteria.

"Do the grills work?" Franklin asked. "Do you cook meals?"

"Yes," the officer responded without slowing his pace. "When we have fresh food."

The thought of a hot meal made Franklin's stomach grumble. Still thinking of food Franklin followed the police officer past the uniform shop, around a corner, and into an office.

"Colonel, this is Major Franklin," the policeman said. "He wants to see you."

Franklin recognized the room. "This was General Gordon's office." Memories of the general bleeding out on the armory floor tore at Franklin's mind.

"Yes, it was his office. I'm Colonel Thompson." The man stood and the two shook hands. "Your medical truck arrived on Tuesday with word that General Gordon died. I've been filling in."

"He was a good man." Franklin nodded. "He died saving other soldiers."

As the police officer departed, Thompson gestured toward a chair.

"I need to brief command on the situation in the Lebanon area." Franklin sat. "Also, I have seven militia prisoners."

"Are they charged with insurrection?" Thompson asked.

Franklin hadn't thought about formal charges. "Yes, I guess that would fit."

"I'll get the JAG officer to draw up papers for you to sign."

"I'll do that." Franklin nodded, hoping it would be done in the next hour. "We also have an insane woman in custody."

"I'm not sure what can be done for her, but I'll ask."

Franklin began his briefing, but Thompson soon held up his hand. "Can you stay until morning? The entire leadership team needs to hear about the militia groups you encountered."

"I believe this unit of Sovereign Militia is neutralized," Franklin said, hoping to expedite his departure.

"Yes, but others have reported a vicious militia group, similar to the one that attacked refugees in the meadow you mentioned. The team needs to hear this new information and I'm hoping your Sovereign Militia prisoners can provide even more intel."

Franklin drew in a deep breath and released it slowly. "We can stay until morning."

"Great." Thompson stood and walked toward the door. "I'll arrange the meeting while you and your soldiers get some needed food and sleep."

Franklin followed Thompson downstairs to the lobby where a soldier stood.

"Sergeant," Thompson said. "Pass down to your relief that I want the leadership team advised that Major Franklin has returned with news about militia groups. Also, have the duty JAG officer notified that we have new prisoners."

"Yes, sir."

Thompson turned his gaze to Franklin. "I'll see you in the morning at 0800?"

Franklin nodded agreement.

Thompson turned and strode down the dark hall.

On the sidewalk outside the building, Keller and Benson were talking. Spotting Franklin, they saluted.

"I've posted guards around the convoy," Keller said. "Most of the other men are finding hot food and warm bunks for the night."

"Show me where," Franklin replied. "I could use that, too."

Together they walked to the intersection.

"They requisitioned a nearby hotel." Keller pointed to the only lighted building down the street. "They'll give you a room for the night."

Inside the building, a restaurant and adjacent conference room now served as a mess hall. Many of his soldiers sat together at long tables, eating a simple stew with buttered bread and drinking water.

Franklin stood in line for his own meal and then sat alone to eat. Days of tension melted away as laughter reached his ears and the smell of meat and broth tickled his nose. Thoughts of home and sleep dominated his mind as he scarfed down the last of his food.

"Good evening, sir."

Franklin looked up as Hansen walked past. "Corporal, come with me, please."

Together they walked out of the building into the darkness.

"Under the martial-law order, you and the rest of the armory squad are now in the regular army." Standing in the empty street, Franklin stopped and faced Hansen. "But what unit you're attached to is uncertain at the moment."

Hansen glanced up and down the street. "The other guys from the armory have asked me about that."

Franklin grinned. "I thought they would. There are two options. We could detach you here or you can return with us to Portland."

"Most of us have family and friends in the Salem area."

Franklin nodded. "I'll inform Colonel Thompson that you'll be joining his command."

"Before you go, sir, I want to tell you how much I appreciate what you did at the armory and in getting Jessica … uh, Private Davis back. You saved all of us."

"That was just part of my job and, while we're talking, there is another job matter we need to discuss. During the battle, you left your position."

"Yes, sir." Hansen nodded. "I was worried about Davis."

"What you did endangered your squad. They might have followed you and exposed themselves to enemy fire, or you might have been captured and then we would have had two hostages. The bottom line is your romantic interest in Private Davis endangered you, your soldiers, and the mission. When you wear that uniform and those chevrons, you must think like a soldier, not like a boyfriend."

"Yes, sir." His head drooped. "I'm sorry, sir."

"Just do better, Corporal."

Both men returned to the hotel, Hansen to the mess area and Franklin to the front desk. "I need a room for the night," he said to the private behind the counter.

"Yes, sir." The soldier saluted. "Officers are on the second floor. There is no running water. However, there are water dispensers and jugs in the bathroom."

Franklin thought about the situation for a moment "What about the toilet?"

"Pour water in it and it'll flush."

Franklin knew that would work, but the sewer pumps and plants weren't functioning. Where would all that wastewater go? He decided he didn't need to know. "What about a key?"

"Your door is unlocked." The private opened a guest book and pointed to where Franklin should sign. "Also, the power for this building will shut down in less than thirty minutes."

As promised, the lights in the room turned on, but the clock by the bed was a windup model. He turned on the television only to view a black lifeless screen. Next, he lifted the phone receiver but heard nothing. Like the TV, perhaps the phone was no more than an ornament from a bygone era. He felt for the phone in his pocket. It might also be a remnant of a bygone era, but at least tonight he could charge it. He plugged in the phone and set it on the nightstand.

Satisfied there would be photos waiting in the morning, Franklin stepped toward the bathroom.

The lights died.

He stopped and stared at the barely visible nightstand. Photos would not be waiting for him in the morning.

Franklin moved to the edge of the bed, took off his uniform, and sniffed it. Though needed, laundry would have to wait. He plopped onto the bed. Certainly he would get home tomorrow, and at least tonight he wouldn't have to lie on the ground.

He closed his eyes and allowed sleep to take him.

Day six

Salem, Oregon, Friday, September 9th

"Sir."

Franklin's eyes flared as he threw off the covers and rocketed to his feet.

The soldier stumbled backward. "Sorry, sir. Colonel Thompson says they're ready for you in the emergency command center."

Light flooded through the nearby window.

Franklin rubbed his eyes. He hadn't wound up the clock. "Thank you, Private. Tell the colonel I'll be there shortly."

The soldier hurried from the room.

Despite what he had said, Franklin took the time to wash his stubble-covered face. After dressing, he hurried down the stairs. Soldiers lined up for what smelled like bacon and eggs. His stomach growled from want, but he had no time for food. Instead, he gulped a cup of coffee and then jogged down the street to the meeting.

In the emergency command center, the huge map of Oregon still dominated one wall, and whiteboards filled another, but the desks and computers had been pushed aside and a large conference table now filled the center of the room.

Colonel Thompson waved him over. "I believe we've all met."

"Yes." Franklin shook hands with the mayor of Salem, the state police superintendent, and the fire marshal. The head of emergency management strode into the room. "Sorry, I'm late. We've been bringing food in from a nearby warehouse. Some has already gone bad, but we think we can salvage most of it."

"Why don't we all sit and get started?" Thompson motioned toward the table and chairs.

Franklin took a seat near the middle of the table. The others moved to the opposite side, except Governor Adams, who sat at the head of the table, staring down at papers in front of him.

"Major Franklin left here with General Gordon to defend the Salem Armory," Colonel Thompson said as he sat. "Please continue from that point."

For the next few minutes, Franklin outlined the events of the last few days, focusing on the battles with the Sovereign Militia and his theory of another group in the Lebanon area.

The mayor leaned forward. "So, the Sovereign Militia couldn't have been the ones that attacked the people in Lebanon?"

"No, not the unit we battled at the armory anyway." Franklin shook his head. "The group that killed the people in the Lebanon meadow had to be another and, I think, a better-trained group. From the time provided by an eyewitness to that attack, the battle at the armory happened at about the same time as the attack in Lebanon."

"There was a witness?" The police superintendent's eyes narrowed.

"Yes," Franklin said. "Neal Evans, a navy vet hiking to his home in Washington State. He believed the attackers had night-vision gear because of the swiftness of the attack and the low number of noncombatant casualties."

Those across from Franklin nodded, but, at the head of the table, the governor continued to stare blankly.

Disconcerted, Franklin looked away.

"Could these attacks have been coordinated?" Thompson asked.

"Possibly." Franklin nodded. "The unit we battled wanted to become an affiliate of the Sovereign Militia. There could be other associated units."

"I believe this meshes well with the reports we've received from other National Guard units and refugees," Thompson said.

"Yes." The mayor sighed.

"We have a serious threat south of the city." The police superintendent shook his head. "More police and soldiers come to us daily, but hunger and thirst are driving many civilians to looting and violence."

"We can't provide for or protect everyone," the mayor added.

Discussion continued for nearly an hour. When it ended, everyone, except the governor, stood and left the room. Thompson escorted Franklin out of the building. As the two approached the convoy, soldiers led the militia prisoners across the lawn toward the building they had just left.

"What will happen to them?" Franklin asked.

"They'll be shot ... well, after we finish interrogating them." Thompson shook Franklin's hand. "Have a safe trip."

*   *   *

Within an hour, the convoy left Salem and headed north along familiar roads toward Portland. A clear blue sky promised a warm day and Franklin could almost imagine that this was a normal drive, except for the abandoned cars and occasional groups of people walking along the freeway edge. The last few days seemed surreal, like a nightmare lingering into wakefulness.

Franklin bit his lip and focused on the here and now. Millions, perhaps billions of people faced dehydration, starvation, and disease. Thinking of humanity so broadly made the problem abstract. His thoughts turned to his own family. As the world collapsed into chaos, how could he protect them? For the rest of the drive north, he struggled to find solutions for basic needs like food and water, but death for millions haunted every idea.

The convoy slowed to a stop at a new wood-and-barbed wire gate near the Portland Cyber Intelligence Center. Three sentries held M4s; another knelt by an M2 machine gun. Keller spoke with the gate guard and within seconds all the vehicles were waved through.

The drivers parked the rigs in the lot next to the center. Franklin stepped from his Humvee as General Sattler emerged from the nearby building.

Franklin saluted.

"I'm glad you're back." The general thrust out his hand and the two shook. "What did you find?"

"Remember the conference call with General Abbott? He stated that you were promoted to brigadier general for the duration of the emergency."

"Yes, of course."

From his pocket Franklin pulled the star patches he had bought from the uniform shop. "You're going to be wearing these for a long time."

General Sattler stared at the patches for several moments. "That conclusion doesn't surprise me." He nodded toward the base office building across the street. "Neal Evans delivered your report yesterday. The situation here is deteriorating rapidly. Gang fights, looting, robbery ... your report and what you just said is a confirmation of our own growing dilemma, but I want to hear your latest news."

The last few words barely pierced Franklin's worried mind. How were Carol and the boys doing? "Uh ... yes, sir. But when I'm done, I'd like to check on my family."

"Certainly." General Sattler nodded. "We're establishing a defensible perimeter and moved your family and others into the secure area."

Franklin sighed in relief and grinned as he followed Sattler into the building.

Just inside, he stopped and stared at a nearby light. "You've got electricity working?"

"Just in this area." Sattler continued down the hall. "We've brought in several additional commercial generators and electricians are working around the clock."

Feeling better about the current situation, Franklin strode to catch up.

*   *   *

Driving a deuce and still wearing the ACUs he had lived in for the last five days, Franklin weaved as he attempted to follow the scratch-paper map the general had drawn.

A bump caused him to look away from the paper as the vehicle rolled onto the sidewalk. Franklin yanked the wheel, steering the vehicle back onto the pavement. "Eyes on the road," he mumbled.

Spotting the desired street sign, he turned left and then into a driveway. Before he could turn off the engine, Carol stepped from the front door onto the porch.

Franklin grabbed a backpack full of MREs and water bottles as he stepped from the truck.

Carol smiled wide and called back through the screen door. "Boys, your dad is home,"

His sons bounded out of the house to greet him. Carol followed the boys at a more demure pace but with an equally welcoming smile.

"Where have you been?" Logan asked. "What happened?"

Franklin hugged his boys. "Let me change and freshen up." He passed the backpack to James. "Here, take this into the house for me."

"How long can you stay?" Carol asked as they embraced.

Mountains of worry tumbled from him as they kissed. "Maybe the weekend." He shrugged. "If things stay calm."

Holding hands, she led him toward the house. "There was a man here yesterday."

"Was his name Neal?"

Carol smiled. "Yes. Thank you for the letter. We were worried." She leaned her head on his shoulder then wrinkled her nose and leaned away. "There's water in the bathroom upstairs if you want to wash up."

Just like the hotel in Salem, Franklin spotted the water jugs in the bathroom. He found his toothbrush and razor on the counter and put them to good use. Then he removed his smelly uniform, stepped into the tub, and gave himself a sponge bath with cold water. When he stood in front of the mirror in clean clothes, he could almost imagine nothing had changed for him and his family—except this wasn't their home.

He toured the four bedrooms upstairs. The chest where they kept the shotgun, pistol, and ammo sat in a corner of the master bedroom. He worked the combination and checked. The shotgun and most of the ammo were inside, but not the pistol.

Many of the trinkets, rugs, and furniture were unfamiliar, but mixed in with them were other pictures, clothing and memorabilia that he did recognize. All of this left him with the feeling of a man stuck in an alternate universe, somewhat familiar but not quite.

Franklin bounded down the stairs and found his family in the living room. "This seems like a good house, bigger than our old one, but how … when did we get it?"

"Lieutenant Poole came by our old home two days ago." Carol brushed back her hair. "He said the owners of this house were visiting Australia, and would probably never return, so the army requisitioned it."

"That makes sense." Franklin nodded, even though he felt bad for the previous occupants. "It wouldn't make sense to leave a home empty when it is within walking distance from the base."

"Then why did you drive the big truck here?" Carol asked with a grin.

"That's our moving truck," Franklin said. "General Sattler told me you had moved closer, but that many of our belongings were still in the old house. I figured we could gather the things we need and want tomorrow."

His sons nodded. "I've gotta get a lot of stuff," Logan said.

"You were supposed to be gone only two days," James said. "What took you so long?"

"The EMP has caused a lot of problems." Those words seemed totally inadequate to the turmoil, hunger, and death he had encountered. After a deep breath, he described the bedlam at the nearby hospital; then he talked about the refugees at the Portland airport with no place to go, but he didn't mention the shooting. He then described how dark Salem had been that first night.

"Darkness is everywhere now." Carol looked out the window. "With so little electricity."

"Do they turn the power off at night?" Franklin asked.

Carol nodded. "Just after sundown for the homes."

"They did the same in Salem." Franklin inhaled a deep breath. "The first night I was there, a nearby armory radioed that they were under attack. We went and ...." There was so much he wanted to say. Carol would want to know how fast civilization was collapsing, but how could he tell her, or the boys, about extracting information from Dick by stabbing him? How could he tell them about all the people who had been murdered or killed ... about the flames and smell of the funeral pyre? Perhaps later, alone with Carol, he could say more. He stared ahead lost in his thoughts.

"I'll get you something to eat."

He smiled, grateful for the diversion.

Later, as Franklin ate, he recalled his imagined meal from yesterday. That breakfast of eggs, toast, bacon, and coffee seemed grand compared with his actual dinner of cold ravioli and an MRE. He threw the remains in the trash as he listened to the boys banter over a chess game. So much had already been lost.

"Dad, will you play the winner?" James asked.

"Tomorrow. Time for bed. Lights out in five minutes, boys." Carol ushered their sons upstairs

Franklin put his plate in the sink. Carol strolled down the stairs, entered the kitchen and kissed her husband.

"Where's the pistol?" Franklin asked.

"You were always one for sweet talk." She leaned close and whispered. "Join me in the bedroom and I'll show you."

With every passing moment, the world fell deeper into the abyss of chaos, hunger, and despair, but as he followed his wife up the stairs, he thanked God for the one thing that really mattered: he and his family were safe.

Day seven

Portland, Oregon, Saturday, September 10th

It might have been a normal early morning drive with the family, except for the pistol on his hip and that he drove a deuce-and-a-half truck. Carol sat beside him. The boys had opted to ride in the back.

The night chill clung to the morning air, but the rising sun shone through the side window as Franklin drove past the steel-and-barbed-wire gate. So much had changed in a week. The small compound of the Cyber Intel Center had expanded to encompass the University of Portland and surrounding neighborhoods. This area, like that in Salem, had limited power and water. Perimeter gates, fences, and walls were under construction around the clock.

The guard waved him through the gate and Franklin turned left along an empty street of shuttered and boarded buildings.

A few blocks later, he turned down a residential street; several people ran from their homes and waved frantically, trying to get him to stop. A man ran at the truck.

Carol gasped.

Franklin yanked the wheel right and missed the man by inches.

A thump came from the back of the truck. James laughed.

"Are you okay?" Carol called over her shoulder.

"Yeah," James shouted. "Logan fell, but he's fine."

Another person stood waving in the street.

Franklin drove around him.

"They're hungry," Carol whispered as she stared at the adults, children, and dogs that dotted the roadside.

"Yes," Franklin replied, keeping a watchful eye for anyone else who might try to stop the truck. His family was a bit hungry, but these people would soon be starving—and they knew it. Leaving the defensive perimeter around the base with his family might have been a mistake. He pressed the gas.

At the back of his mind, a thought niggled like a thorn, painful and irritating. How soon would hunger turn to desperation, chaos, and rioting? He would keep his family close to home, and as safe as he could.

"There's the street." Carol pointed.

Torn from thought, Franklin pulled the wheel hard to the left, inducing another thud and a laugh from James.

Franklin backed the deuce into his driveway and parked. As he stepped from the vehicle, Ted hurried over from next door.

"How come that truck works, but so many others don't?" his neighbor asked.

"Hi, Ted. Good to see you." Franklin forced a grin.

"Oh, yeah. Hi, Dirk. Glad to see you're okay."

"You too, Ted. I don't know the details, but military vehicles are built to withstand EMPs." Franklin turned to Carol as she helped the boys from the back of the truck.

"Hi, Dirk." Another neighbor joined them, but, unable to recall his name, Franklin just smiled and nodded.

Carol passed the house key to the boys and they ran to the house, then she smiled and greeted both neighbors.

"How are you doing for food?" Ted asked.

"None here," Franklin interjected. He had no intention of telling Ted about the backpack full of food and water he had brought to the other house, or the remaining supplies Carol had taken from this one.

"I still have some food, but a lot of it will spoil soon."

"Your frozen stuff?" Carol asked. "I thought you had a generator."

"He does," the other neighbor interjected.

What was his name? Franklin stared, but couldn't remember.

"Ted's been sharing power with others. Running extension cords to my house and others, but it uses more gas.

"I'm low on gas." Ted frowned.

"Eat what you can," Carol suggested.

"I barbequed some three days ago and used all the briquettes I had."

"Use our barbeque." Carol smiled and turned to her husband.

He had bought the propane grill last summer and had three full canisters that would probably never be refilled. "Use it."

"Thanks." Ted smiled. "Several people have food that will go bad, I'll see if we can get a few other grills and organize a neighborhood barbeque. Bring what you have. You're all invited."

Ted and the other man hurried across the street before Franklin could object. All he wanted was to move his family to safety and then relax with them for a few precious hours. He had no interest in attending a block party.

Carol waved to the neighbors gathering across the street, and then she clasped Franklin's hand and gave it a gentle squeeze as they stepped toward the house. "Ted is doing the same thing we are."

"I'm not annoying anyone."

She giggled. "He's just trying to survive. We should help."

Franklin drew a deep breath. "What can we do?"

The boys bounded out the front door. Each held a box brimming with trophies, models, games, and baseball bats.

"I know what you're thinking." Carol opened the screen door. "The games might be useful."

"Maybe even the baseball bat." Franklin grinned.

Inside, Carol stopped him. "Could the base spare some gasoline for Ted's generator, or maybe some food?"

He shook his head. "I doubt there's any extra food, and the modern army runs on fuel, but I might be able to help Ted and some of our other neighbors."

Carol cast him a questioning glance.

"The general is converting an empty warehouse into temporary housing. He's starting to bring in electricians, plumbers, carpenters, and others with needed skills."

"Ted is an insurance actuary." Carol shook her head. "Ron manages a department store. I don't know what Bill did, but he's retired."

"I'll see about getting some gas."

For the rest of the morning, the family filled the truck with boxes of belongings. Just past noon, Franklin walked out the front door with the last load.

Ted strolled over and stared into the truck. "Did you hear about the murders on the next block?"

"No." Franklin pushed the last box into the back, leaving just enough space for his sons to sit during the return trip.

"An old couple was killed and the house ransacked. I think they were looking for food. We can hear gunfire every night now." Ted sighed. "I'm glad Carol and the boys are safe."

"Safe has always been a relative term." Franklin leaned on the tailgate. "They'll be safer, but is anyone safe?"

"No." Ted shook his head. "A lot more people are going to die." His eyes were sad, but his gaze held firm. "Most of us aren't going to make it through the winter … I've run risk assessments for many years; I know that the odds are I won't see next spring."

"No one knows the future." For the first time, Franklin felt a connection with Ted. "We've all just got to do the best that we can and hope … maybe pray a lot more than we have in the past."

"I agree." Ted nodded slowly. "I hope you come to the block party this afternoon."

"Thanks." Franklin forced a grin on his face as he pulled the keys from his pocket. "The grill is on the back porch, and the gate is unlocked." He paused for a moment. "I'm going to try to come back later with gasoline for you."

"That would be a big help."

Carol and James exited the house, followed by Logan wearing a football helmet and pads. Both the boys ran past her and jumped into the back of the truck.

"Goodbye, Ted." Carol shook his hand and then climbed into the cab.

Franklin said his own goodbye, shut the tailgate, and drove the deuce away.

*   *   *

When everything from the truck had been moved into the new house, Franklin plopped onto the couch. They still had to decide where most things would go and what from the previous owner needed to be removed, but that could wait. Did any of the MREs he brought contain coffee? He would rest a few moments and then check. This certainly wasn't the quiet weekend with family he wanted.

Carol walked into the living room and dropped beside him. "I hate moving."

He hugged her. "Were you going to tell me about the murder near our home or the nightly shooting sprees?"

"Near the old house?" She turned just enough to look at him. "Darn Ted." She sighed. "No, we had already moved when you returned. Why say—"

"I should know."

"Telling you wouldn't do any good. You know what the world is like now. You've seen worse."

"I'm supposed to protect—"

"Yes, but when you're out defending the world, I'm left to protect our boys and our home. And I try not to worry you during those times."

"This is different."

Carol nodded. "It is, but you're still going to leave me behind and I'll have to deal with home and family."

They snuggled close. She had always been so strong and confident. He kissed her and she kissed him back.

A giggle erupted from the entrance to the room. Their youngest son disappeared down the hall.

Franklin grinned and kissed his wife again.

"We could go somewhere more private." Carol smiled.

"I'll need a raincheck on that. I'm going to see if I can get Ted some gas. I want to deliver it and be back here by lights out."

"I'll be waiting."

*   *   *

"How much gasoline are we talking about?" General Sattler asked.

Franklin hesitated. With careful use, twenty or thirty gallons could last Ted and the other neighbors for several weeks, but no new fuel would be refined for years. Eventually, everyone would run out. How much could the base spare?

"Are you thinking a barrel … forty-two gallons?" the general asked.

"Yes, that's about right. I know we can't help everyone but—"

"Right now we have more supply than we can store or stabilize."

Franklin cast him a confused glance.

"All the fuel that had been produced to run a modern economy is still sitting in tanks, but now there are only a few vehicles and generators running. So, take a barrel. I'll write the order for the quartermaster."

At the fuel depot, Franklin helped the private pump gasoline into a drum, spilling some on his sleeve and hands. Together they loaded the barrel into the back of the same deuce he had been driving all day.

Fumes irritated his nose as Franklin slowed to a stop at the gate next to the guard. In the direction of his old home, thick black smoke hung over the nearby buildings. He leaned out the window of the truck and pointed to the dark column. "Private, do you know what happened?"

"No, sir. But we've been seeing a lot of fires lately."

Smoke masked the smell of fumes as Franklin raced the truck toward his previous house. Near the old neighborhood, dark billows rose as if from a volcano. When he turned onto the street, a fully engulfed home came into view. Cinders landed on the nearby homes.

Just ahead, the sprawled body of a man blocked his way. Several grills lay toppled on the pavement nearby. Franklin braked to a stop. A group of men he didn't recognize stood at the far end of the street, staring at the truck.

Who were these men? How did the fire start? Where had everyone gone? Franklin unsnapped his holster and stepped out with the pistol in hand.

In the distance a woman screamed.

At a casual pace, the men disappeared into the swirling smoke.

"Hi, Dirk. You shouldn't have come back." Ted sat leaning against the rail of his front porch. A red stain ran from his abdomen to a puddle on the step.

Franklin grabbed a first-aid kit and ran to his neighbor. "What happened? No, don't talk." Franklin cut away the shirt and found a bullet wound with no exit.

"They smelled the food. Came like wolves. We tried to stop them."

"Who attacked you?" Franklin asked as he cleaned the injury.

"I don't know. A gang. Ten or twelve of them."

Franklin bandaged and wrapped Ted's wound. "Can you walk? I don't think I can carry you to the truck."

"Leave me."

"No." Franklin helped Ted to his feet, but then he collapsed, pulling them both to the ground. "Stay with me, Ted!" Franklin searched for a pulse.

He didn't find one.

Day eight

Portland, Oregon, Sunday, September 11th

Franklin watched Carol sleep as the morning sun warmed the room. Her mouth hung open and her hair splayed in every direction. He smiled. This moment of quiet peace, gazing at the woman he loved, was exactly what he needed.

He wanted to stroke her disheveled hair, hug and kiss her, but that would disturb this now-perfect moment that lingered between a traumatic past and uncertain future.

In the quiet of the morning, he heard his sons talking as they descended the stairs.

"Are Mom and Dad up?" Logan asked.

"I don't think so," James replied. "I heard Dad come in late last night."

"What time is it?" Carol whispered with her eyes still closed.

"Early." Franklin brushed her hair with his hand. "Just rest."

Her tranquility lent peace to the morning as he continued to watch the gentle rise and fall of her breasts.

Westminster chimes from a nearby church rang out the hour.

Carol's eyes fluttered open. "I should get up."

"Or we could stay here—forever." He leaned over and kissed her.

"Seven in the morning?"

"You counted the chimes?"

"Yes." Carol sat up. "The boys need breakfast. We need to get more things from the old house."

He clutched her hand. "We won't be getting anything else from the other home."

"What? Why?" Her eyes widened. "You were so late getting back last night. What happened?"

Franklin told her about bringing gasoline to Ted and finding a house at the end of the street ablaze. "A group of men stood in a cluster nearby."

"Who were they?"

"I think they were part of a gang. Ted said they smelled the food and attacked like a pack of wolves."

Carol gasped. "How is Ted and everyone else?"

He hesitated, trying to think of a good way to phrase his answer, but there wasn't a good way. "He was shot during the confrontation."

She covered her mouth with a hand.

"I tried to help him ... but he died. The fire spread along the street, but I think everyone else had already fled."

Carol sat on the edge of the bed. "I suggested the barbeque." Tears rolled down her cheeks. "It's my fault Ted died. My fault ... all of it."

Franklin hugged her tight. "You're a good person. It isn't your fault that bad people do evil things."

After the tears subsided, Carol wiped her eyes. "I've tried to be strong for you, but this has been a really hard week."

"It's been hard for everyone. The world is falling apart, but you've managed this family very well."

Carol looked toward a window for a long moment. "Can we go to church?"

The idea caught Franklin off guard. Carol had attended church as a child, but he had rarely set foot in one. His surprise must have shown on his face.

"What else would we do this morning?" Carol shrugged her shoulders.

Franklin thought of many things he'd rather do, but Carol needed comfort and so he smiled. "Sure, let's go to church."

She squeezed his hand. "You're a good husband."

Later, after an MRE breakfast of crackers, peanut butter, hash-brown potatoes, and fruit punch, Franklin announced, "We're going to church."

"Huh?" James' eyes narrowed. "Is someone getting married?"

"Or did they die?" Logan's eyes flared wide.

"Neither," Carol replied. "Your father and I think it would be a good idea."

"Why?" Logan protested.

"They're afraid you're going to hell." James grinned at him.

"Watch your language." Carol gave her son an annoyed stare.

"Come on." James grabbed his brother's arm. "Let's get you dressed for eternity."

"Huh?" Logan's eyes narrowed in confusion as James led him away.

When they were alone, Franklin turned to his wife. "I expected more resistance from James."

"Something is going on with him." Carol shook her head. "But let's get ready."

Unsure what to wear, Franklin dressed in a business suit that seemed to fit better than the last time he wore it. Carol donned a green dress and heels. The boys tromped downstairs in slacks and collared shirts.

"Oh," Carol gushed. "You both look so handsome."

"James made me wear this." Logan scowled.

Staring at them, Franklin asked, "Who are you and what have you done with my sons?"

"Very funny, Dad." James continued toward the door. "Let's go."

Confused by his son's hurry, Franklin cast his wife a questioning glance.

She shrugged.

Everyone seemed to be walking in the same direction and Franklin took interest in how everyone dressed as they strolled along the street and sidewalks toward the church three blocks away. Franklin recognized only a few of the men, but Carol waved and talked to many of the families.

"How do you know these people?" he asked.

"I go to the PTA meeting, attend the wives club, and help out with Cub Scouts and Boy Scouts."

"Oh." He nodded.

As they neared the church the homes were larger, with more spacious lawns and older, larger trees. Around the next corner, the church came into view. He had passed the old brick building countless times but, other than the park-like setting around it, had never given it much thought. Now he had many questions about the church and God, but Logan gave voice to the first.

"Did God break everything? Did he do this to us?"

"No," Franklin replied as they climbed the steps to the entrance. "Of course not."

"Then who did it?"

"I'll explain later." But the thought nagged at Franklin as he continued toward the large wooden front doors. *Did you strike out at us, God?*

James led the way across the large lawn. Four lancet-style stained glass windows brightened the side of the building. A wooden steeple rested on the top where the bell rang out the nine o'clock hour.

Franklin followed his son up ten stone steps and through large wooden doors into a lobby-like area. Beyond that, another set of wooden doors stood open to the sanctuary where a vaulted ceiling hung above white walls. The windows provided both color and ample illumination.

Franklin estimated that about a hundred people filled the majority of the pews. He would have been content to sit in one of the empty spots toward the rear, but the rest of the family followed James toward a half-empty row near the center. After everyone had slid into place, James gave a slight wave to a blonde-haired girl two rows ahead. She smiled and waved back.

The confusing behavior of their adolescent son snapped into clarity. The young lady must be Emma. Franklin turned to his wife with a grin and she smiled back at him.

A man in his mid-thirties, with brown hair, stood at the front of the church. "Hello everyone. I'm Steve Duncan, the lead pastor here. I recognize many of your faces, but if this isn't your usual church, know that in these tumultuous times we are here for you and you are welcome in this house of God. Let's stand and make a joyful noise to the Lord."

They stood along with the choir and Carol handed Franklin a hymnal as he pretended to sing several unfamiliar hymns.

When the choir sat, Pastor Duncan approached the lectern. "Thomas Paine described the early days of the American revolution as 'the times that try men's souls.' We are once again in such a time. All of us are confused and worried, but the Lord is our rock, our refuge. He knows that in this time of trouble, we are crying out to him. He does hear us and he will guide us."

Franklin didn't know what guidance God could or would provide. He had read only bits and pieces of the Bible and didn't think he owned one.

"… is my rock, my fortress; in him I take refuge…"

Were these quotes from the Bible or merely pretty prose? Spotting a Bible on the back of the pew in front of him, Franklin grabbed it.

"The book of Zechariah was written during a time of despair …"

Carol flipped it open to the table of contents and pointed to Zechariah. Franklin found the book and began flipping through the pages.

"… Zechariah says the Lord will comfort us."

Franklin couldn't find what the pastor was quoting but discovered other verses in Zechariah.

And it shall come to pass in all the land, says the Lord, that two-thirds in it shall be cut off and die, but one-third shall be left in it: I will bring the one-third through the fire, will refine them as silver is refined, and test them as gold is tested.

A chill ran through Franklin as the implication of the words hit him. He knew that two-thirds of the population might die in the coming year through a combination of starvation, violence, and disease. Had the EMP been some sort of spiritual testing? Did the verses actually refer to that or was it mere coincidence? He didn't know, and he hated not knowing.

"But until that time we need to focus on the important things: faith, family, and friends." Pastor Duncan closed his Bible and ended with a prayer.

People around him stood and stepped from the pews.

Carol leaned over and smiled. "That was a very comforting sermon, don't you think?"

Franklin forced a grin. "I'm glad we came." He held on to the Bible as he left the pew. James held back, talking with the blonde girl.

As they departed, Carol shook the pastor's hand. "Your sermon gave me comfort."

"I'm glad."

Holding out the Bible, Franklin asked, "May I borrow this?"

"Yes. Keep it. I wish more people would take them."

An old man tapped Franklin on the shoulder. "Read it, young man. The Great Tribulation has arrived."

*   *   *

Franklin sat on the front porch later that day, drinking a packet of MRE apple juice and reading the last chapter of Zechariah. In the distance, he heard the rumble of an engine.

The Humvee turned down his street.

Franklin swore and set the Bible on a table.

The Humvee stopped in front of his home and Sergeant Keller climbed out of the vehicle and saluted.

"I hope you've had a good weekend, sir."

"I've enjoyed the time with my family." Franklin knew the medical truck had returned from the armory with the wounded but hadn't heard if they picked up Keller's wife and child as planned. "Is your family well?"

"Yes, sir."

"Great, but I don't think you came here to discuss family morale. Is there a problem?"

"The general told me two things. He wants me to get the squads ready for another mission."

Carol strolled from the house with a frown.

"What else did the general say?" Franklin asked.

"He wants to see you first thing in the morning for the pre-mission brief."

Day nine

Portland, Oregon, Monday, September 12th

Franklin arrived early the next morning, entered the conference room, and flipped the light switch. As fluorescent bulbs flickered on, the rich aroma of coffee tickled his nose. Lights and coffee were such normal things, but yet now so unusual. He drew in a deep breath of familiar flavor as he filled a cup.

Steps drew closer behind him.

"Oh, good morning, sir."

Franklin turned and greeted Lieutenant Poole. "Do you know what this meeting is about?"

"Yes." Poole nodded. "Yesterday a civilian came to us with information on the location of several large warehouses of —"

Another man, dressed in a business suit and tie, entered the room. He stood off by himself and made no attempt at conversation. Both today and Sunday such formal civilian attire had struck him as unusual, even otherworldly.

Poole looked Franklin in the eye and gave a slight nod toward the door, indicating they should step out. Before they could, General Sattler strode into the conference room.

"Good, I'm glad you're all here. Major, have you met our newest resident?"

"I was just about to," Franklin said and held out his hand. "I'm Major Dirk Franklin."

"Nice to meet you. I'm Brad Burton with the Multnomah County Planning Department."

"Let's get this meeting started." The general unfurled a large map of northern Oregon on the table. "Lieutenant, get me something to hold this down."

Poole brought coffee mugs and when the map lay in place at one end of the table, the four looked on as the general continued. "Yesterday, Brad brought us information on five large warehouses outside of Portland. These buildings contain food and other supplies that we need. I've ordered the requisition of the supplies under the martial law decree. Platoons have already been dispatched to three of them." He pointed to those locations on the map. "I need your platoon to secure this regional distribution center east of the city."

"Do we have enough soldiers to adequately secure those locations *and* this base?" Franklin asked.

"No, but I don't see that we have a choice." Sattler shook his head. "The fresh and refrigerated food will have gone bad, but I want you to transport the rest here. With supplies from all five warehouses, we should have enough to survive and bring in others we need to establish a viable community."

Thinking of the manpower needed to protect all the warehouses and the base, Franklin shook his head.

"I brought you this information so we could feed the city," Burton's eyes narrowed. "We should be setting up food distribution centers."

"We'll be able to feed more people when we have these supplies," the general said.

"But with your plan, most people won't be fed." Burton turned and walked several steps away. "Thousands will starve."

"This base is the only island of law and order in northern Oregon," Franklin said in frustration. "What would you have us do?"

"Feed everyone while you fix the power grid and restore order."

"For the foreseeable future, that's impossible." Poole's eyes narrowed.

"Then what sort of future do you foresee?" Burton asked.

"Over the next year?" Poole shook his head. "Death—on a massive scale."

Franklin cringed at the words but had reached the same conclusion.

"No!" Burton rested his head on his hands. "I refuse to believe that."

"Most crops can't be planted until spring and nothing is being imported, but millions of people are in need of food." Poole scowled at Burton. "If we survive until spring, we'll need fuel for farm equipment and large areas of farmland. Do you know how to raise crops on the scale we need? Do you know how to restore the power grid? Do you—"

General Sattler held up his hand. "Thank you, Lieutenant, for that accurate but grim assessment. We need time—time to gather equipment and people together while we learn the needed skills to restore civilization."

"Millions will die while you learn. What kind of people are you that you can accept this level of catastrophe?" Burton asked.

The general stared at Burton with a stone-cold face. "While we are learning how to restore civilization, just remember that your family was brought inside the perimeter in exchange for this information. You and your family will be fed, while we struggle to establish a viable community."

"But in the meantime, who decides who lives and who dies?"

"For now, I do," Sattler turned to Franklin. "You have your orders."

*　　　*　　　*

An hour later, Franklin was back at home, packing the last few items he would need. When he finished, he set the Bible on top.

"How long will you be gone?" Carol asked.

Franklin locked the duffel bag. "Not long. A week maybe."

She pulled him close and rested her head on his chest. "I remember when short deployments passed so quickly, but that last one dragged on so very long."

At the sound of a vehicle, Franklin glanced out the window.

Logan ran past the open bedroom door. "A Humvee just turned onto our street." He thundered down the stairs.

"You really think Dad doesn't know?" James asked as he walked past.

The vehicle stopped in front of Franklin's home. He threw his bag over a shoulder, kissed Carol, hugged the boys, and joined Sergeant Keller in the Humvee for the ride back to the operations center.

"Lieutenant Poole had us pack a lot of gear." Keller turned onto the main road. "Are you expecting more trouble on this mission?"

"No, but I want to be overprepared. Look what happened last time on our information-gathering jaunt to the airport and Salem."

"Okay." Keller nodded. "We have night-vision gear and plenty of ammo."

At the operations center on base, soldiers stood in formation in front of two Humvees, three deuces, and a fueler parked to one side. On the other end of the lot, a dozen additional trucks, both military and civilian, waited.

"Attention," Poole ordered.

Franklin stepped from the Humvee. "At ease." He moved to the front of the formation. "Our mission is simple, secure a distribution center so the food inside can be transported back here. Those of you who have been with me in the past know that events can turn violent in a second. So, move quickly but stay sharp." He pointed to a dozen trucks parked nearby that ranged in size from three semi-trucks down to large vans. "When we've finished transporting the food back here, I want all of us home safe."

"Hooah," the soldiers shouted.

The platoon pulled out with Keller again driving the deuce with a plow blade. Franklin followed in a Humvee with Private Thomas and other soldiers.

Recalling the wound Thomas endured at the armory, Franklin asked, "How's your leg?"

"It's in a brace. I can walk—slowly."

Normally the walking wounded wouldn't be sent on missions, but they were short of soldiers and Thomas could sit and drive. Franklin would have preferred a company of soldiers for this operation, but at least the platoon stood at full strength, two squads of fifteen soldiers each. Most were combat veterans, having fought with him in Salem and south of Lebanon, with a few new people mixed in.

The lead deuce turned right and Keller slammed his first abandoned vehicle of the day to the side of the road. Three hours later, the convoy rumbled down a lonely two-lane road through rolling hills and farmland. Low in the sky, the sun shone on Franklin's face. A man riding a horse with a rifle slung over his back waved as they passed.

"Where is this place we're going?" a soldier asked. "I don't see anything that looks like a warehouse?"

"Yeah, aren't we supposed to be there by now?" another asked.

"Enjoy the ride." Franklin looked over his shoulder at the soldiers in the rear seat. "When we secure the place, you'll be loading trucks for days."

"How will we tell the other trucks we're ready for them to come?" Thomas asked. "We're out of radio range."

"You're going to tell the base." Franklin smiled at his driver.

"Huh, sir?"

"When we've found and secured the center, we'll load up the three deuces we have. You'll lead them back to base and return with all the other trucks. Meanwhile, we'll try to get any of the trucks there to work."

Thomas nodded. "Sounds like a good plan."

"I'm glad you approve." Franklin grinned.

Minutes later, the radio crackled. "I think I see a warehouse on the south side of the road ahead."

The land all around him looked the same, flat and largely empty, but Franklin pulled out his binoculars and looked where Keller had indicated. There, at the edge of the horizon, a mammoth gray structure seemed to emerge from the Earth.

As they grew closer, a stone wall obscured the lower part of the two- or three-story building, but the upper portion of the structure was now visible. During the meeting, Burton had described the place as a large distribution center, but the side of this structure wasn't large—it was huge, possibly more than a thousand feet long.

"We're going to need a lot of trucks," a soldier said.

Franklin agreed.

When the convoy cleared the stone wall, a smaller building, closer to the road, came into view, with a parking area along the front and far side. A sign over the door read, "Personnel and Employment Office."

"Pull into the parking lot," he ordered over the radio. "We'll recon the area from there."

The vehicles rolled off the road and into the lot. Two of the deuces pulled ahead and parked near the side of the building. Franklin stepped from the Humvee. A hint of wood smoke reached his nose along with distant voices.

The driver of one of the Humvees pointed toward the main building. "What's going on there?"

Franklin strode to the corner of the office. Someone had placed a bench under an awning at the side of the building. But his gaze shifted almost at once to the warehouse, still a quarter mile away, but now fully in view. Using binoculars for a better view, he scanned the area. In the meadow between them and the warehouse, hundreds, perhaps thousands of people circulated among tents, tarps, campfires and a few old trucks and cars. The tents ranged from small two-person pup tents to large family and army surplus types. Between the camp and the warehouse was a wide swath of empty grassland. As Franklin watched, some in the camp pointed in his direction. Then, like stampeding cattle, they ran toward him.

"Back in the vehicles!" Franklin ran toward his Humvee. "Go back the way we came until I say stop."

As the convoy pulled away, Franklin looked over his shoulder. Most of the mob had slowed to a walk. Although they were now less threatening, memories of the airport shooting compelled him to leave. He unfolded his map and looked for a good location to set up camp and recon the situation.

Franklin decided to rendezvous at a gas station about a mile from the warehouse. After passing the information to Keller, Franklin leaned back in his seat. Why did the crowd just linger near the fence? They had the numbers to tear it down and take the food. Why had they run at the convoy?

*   *   *

Later that day, Franklin divided the soldiers into Alpha and Bravo Troops, with Lieutenant Poole in charge of Bravo. Then, after dark, Franklin took Alpha on a hike across the fields to the rear of the distribution center. He led the squad into a gully where he and Keller donned night-vision gear. A hundred yards of level ground stood between them and the warehouse, but both darkness and waist-high pasture grass might hide them as they approached the complex.

"Keller, stay on my left. Everyone else spread out along the back of the building as we approach," Franklin whispered as he peered into the green-tinted darkness. "Report back if you see anything."

For nearly a minute, they crept closer.

Franklin gazed along the fence but saw no one.

"I see movement on the roof," Keller pointed.

Lifting his gaze, Franklin spotted three people. Then a flash, like a bright new star, lit his goggle.

Keller swore and fell to the ground.

Day ten

Rural Oregon, Tuesday, September 13th

Franklin glanced through his night-vision gear. "Snipers on the roof!" Then he grabbed Keller by the jacket. A sticky wetness dampened his hand. "Return fire," he shouted to the squad.

Keller staggered to his feet.

With his M4 in one hand, Franklin wrapped the other arm around his wounded comrade. The metallic smell of blood prickled his nostrils. "Are you okay?"

"Not sure…think so." Keller's words were slurred.

Several soldiers fired blindly into the dark. All of them remained exposed. "Regroup at the gully."

Holding tight to Keller, Franklin ran to the ravine. "Medic! Everyone hold your fire."

Bickel arrived and hovered over Keller as she examined him with a red penlight.

Through the binoculars of his night-vision gear, Franklin focused on the warehouse. Four people knelt in separate positions along the back wall. Another person walked from one spot to the next. Franklin steadied the M4 on a rock. This wasn't a sniper rifle, but if two people were close and he fired a three-round burst, he might, even at this distance, hit one of them. "How's Keller?"

Bickel's voice was barely a whisper. "He has a deep laceration along the—"

"I'll be okay, sir."

Keller's words were still muddled, but Franklin nodded. "Good." Then he turned his attention back to the warehouse. As he stared through the scope, the walker on the roof drew close to one of the snipers. When they were beside each other, Franklin fired.

Both dropped out of sight.

Franklin took a deep breath. He wasn't sure he had killed or even wounded anyone, but those on the roof now hunkered low. Satisfied he had made his point and bought the squad a few moments to evade, he led Alpha Troop back to the convoy.

*   *   *

In the glow of early morning light, Franklin watched as Corporal Bickel removed the bandage on Keller's face. A cut ran deep along his right cheek. "You're going to have a scar and a great story to tell your kid."

Bickel removed scissors, forceps, thread, and needle from her bag. "Hop onto the truck tailgate and lie down." Keller did as directed and the medic gave him a shot. "In a minute, you won't feel any pain. You were lucky. If the bullet had been a little bit to the left, you'd be dead."

Keller winced. "Little to the right…it would've missed."

A moment later, Lieutenant Poole approached with his gaze on Keller. "Nasty cut."

A lopsided grin spread across Keller's face.

"Hold still. Don't talk and try not to grin." Bickel stitched.

Franklin motioned for Poole to step away. "Send Private Thomas and Rankin back to base in one of the Humvees with my report."

Poole nodded. "Do you want to send Keller back also?"

"No. His wound isn't serious and we're going to need him when we attack the warehouse. "I'm asking the general to send reinforcements, sniper rifles, and more breaching equipment. Until we take the warehouse, I plan to keep whoever is in there pinned down and afraid to go out."

"Could the people inside be military or police?"

"I don't think so. They were quick to shoot and willing to watch those outside the perimeter fence starve."

"What are you going to do about all those civilians, sir?"

Franklin sighed. "We need to talk with them." His orders were to bring the food back, which would leave the civilians to starve. A lot of people were going to die of hunger. There was little he could do about the world, but if they seized the warehouse, he might be able to help these people—a little.

*   *   *

James Franklin sat hiding in a cluster of bushes with Emma. The only sound was the splash of water from the nearby creek that ran through the small park. The world might be falling apart, but in a few ways, his life had turned for the better. School hadn't reopened and his new home inside the base perimeter was only a couple of blocks from Emma's house. He had seen her nearly every day this week. Times like this, alone together, were the best part of his day. Sometimes they talked and sometimes, like now, they just sat and smiled at each other. He drank water from a canteen and passed her the last of his late afternoon cracker-and-cheese lunch.

Several moments passed as she finished every morsel. "I should probably get back before Dad hunts me down."

Looking at the crumb-free plate, he frowned. "Are you getting enough to eat?"

"Is anyone?"

James shook his head. "But you live on the base. Your dad is a police officer. Don't you get food?"

"Some." She looked at him with sad eyes. "They say that most of it is kept by the military."

James raised an eyebrow. "No, I don't believe that. Things are getting back to normal. They say school will restart soon." He grinned. "You said you wanted to be a cheerleader."

"That was a silly dream. I'm not that girl anymore." Her eyes flared wide and her voice rose. "They talk about reopening school, but it hasn't happened, and even if it does, do you really think they'll have a football or basketball team? Do you think there will be cheerleaders? Let's face it. I'm never going to be a veterinarian and you won't be a pilot."

They would need vets for farm animals. James thought she had a good chance to become one, but with almost all electronics fried by the EMP the chances of him becoming a fighter pilot were slim. Their silence hung heavy between them for a moment. "Thinking about the future is pointless right now. My parents try to plan, but really they just want to make it through each day."

"How can we live like that?"

"We just do, I guess." James shrugged.

Gunfire erupted nearby. A woman screamed.

James held Emma down with his arm as he peered over the bush. "Stay down. Stay quiet."

*   *   *

Later that afternoon, Dirk Franklin took a squad of soldiers with him in a Humvee and headed toward the employment office near the warehouse.

Along the way, one soldier asked, "Sir, what are the rules of engagement if shooting starts?"

"Return fire and protect yourselves as you retreat to the Humvee, but I want to try and talk with them."

"They didn't seem very talkative the last time we were there, sir," another soldier said.

Franklin nodded. It had spooked him when the crowd surged toward them yesterday. "Deploy in a line facing them with rifles at the ready."

"Hooah," rippled through the Humvee.

They arrived and deployed as ordered with Franklin standing in the middle, facing the warehouse more than four hundred yards away. Was it possible that today even more people were encamped in the meadow? His gut wrenched. This would go well only if the people were willing to talk and listen. Any other response and the situation could turn ugly very quickly.

A roar erupted from the crowd about a hundred yards away and, like cattle, they stampeded in Franklin's direction. Taking a deep breath, he strode forward and held out one hand in a stop gesture. The other hand rested on his holster. "Stop and we can talk." *This is useless. I'm going to get myself and these soldiers killed.*

"Stop! Let's talk," he repeated, wishing he had a megaphone.

The soldiers stepped forward and stiffened, ready to fire.

The crowd slowed and came to a restless halt about twenty yards from the line of soldiers. More than a hundred men stood along the front of the throng. Most were armed and many had their weapons aimed in his direction. Behind them were women and children. Every one of them looked anxious, afraid, and desperate.

One man stepped forward. "Are you here to help us or them?"

Franklin wasn't there to help either group. His orders were clear and simple: secure the food and transport it back to the base. But as he gazed at the hungry and desperate crowd, an idea formed. "Perhaps we can help each other."

The man pointed to the bench beside the employment office. There, far enough away for a private conversation but still in sight of both soldiers and civilians, they sat.

"I'm Major Dirk Franklin."

"Ryan Hill." They shook hands. "So are you with the real army or a militia group?"

"I'm with the United States Army."

Ryan shook his head. "I was beginning to think there wasn't such a thing anymore."

"We've been busy, but we still exist."

"It doesn't take great deductive insight to determine you're here for the food."

Franklin nodded.

"I can't let you take it."

"I didn't think you had control of the warehouse."

"I don't yet, but," Ryan gestured toward the other civilians, "we will soon."

"Many of you will die if you attack the building."

"Yes." Ryan nodded. "But we'll starve to death if we don't." He took a deep breath and continued. "There are only thirty or forty people inside. We have many more with guns." He grinned. "And I was the manager of the warehouse and have all the keys."

Franklin foresaw many problems. From the recon mission last night, he surmised that the group inside the warehouse had night-vision gear, rifles, and at least some training. Did they have military weapons? Had they barricaded the doors? He would have. Other questions came to mind, but he simply smiled and said, "Let's try to work together. For a start, who are the guys inside?"

"I don't know for sure." Ryan shrugged. "They showed up two days after the sun storm. They had uniforms and insisted they were there under government orders, but then they killed a couple of security guards. The few of us who were in the warehouse ran for our lives.

"Five days later I ran out of food at home and so I came here with my wife and kids." Ryan stared at the warehouse. "We've managed to get some food from town and hunting, but the camp grows daily." He stared at the massive distribution center. "There's enough stuff in that building for all of us, but I can't wait much longer."

"They're surrounded," Franklin said. "They must know that. Perhaps we can convince them to leave."

"I don't think so," Ryan said grimly. "I inherited this leadership job after a couple of others tried to talk their way in—and got shot. Like I said, we're going to take the food but not with words."

"Perhaps talk and a show of force could push them out." Franklin told Ryan about the rifles, reinforcements, and breaching equipment he had requested from the base. "The only way I see this ending is with them leaving, but if we have to fight, many of my soldiers will be wounded or killed, and even more of your people."

"They won't leave. Our choice is to attack or starve."

"Then work with me until the additional soldiers and equipment arrive. We might be able to do this with significantly less carnage. Do you have a map of the building?"

"Yes." Ryan called for one of his men to retrieve it.

Together they moved back to the Humvee for planning.

"I want a sign painted." Franklin held his arms wide. "Two yards long on plywood and set on poles. We ask them for a dialogue. If that doesn't work, then we shoot."

Ryan grinned. "Standard plywood size is four by eight."

Franklin rolled his eyes. "Can someone in your group make it?"

"Sure, but it won't work." He left and talked to one of his men and then returned. "Your sign will be up in about an hour."

Franklin and Ryan discussed plans and the placement of both soldiers and civilians until a dozen men walked across the field into the no-man's land beyond the camp. Two carried posthole diggers, while the others held poles and a large sheet of plywood. One side glistened white with red lettering.

Franklin glimpsed a couple of words but wasn't sure what it said. He asked Ryan, "What exactly did you tell them to say on the sign?"

"The U.S. Army is here. Talk or we start shooting."

Franklin gritted his teeth. It was what he had said, but not exactly what he wanted on the sign.

The holes were easily dug in the soft dry ground and the sign nailed in place.

Bang!

The sign shuddered. Splinters flew.

The crowd scattered.

More shots thundered as the soldiers hurried to find cover.

"Well, at least they read it." Franklin jumped into one of the Humvees with Ryan and moved it behind the personnel building. There, they exited the vehicle and used its hood as a table while they continued to plan. "I suggest a diversion over here." He pointed to the far end of the warehouse. "Then we attack at these loading bays. The semi-trucks will provide cover and, with breaching equipment, we can be inside the building in seconds."

Between rifle shots, an engine roared.

Franklin looked over his shoulder. A Humvee raced along the road, turned into the parking lot, and screeched to a stop. Private Rankin jumped out and rendered a quick salute.

Franklin returned it and glanced at the empty Humvee. "Where's Thomas and the reinforcements?"

"Thomas is dead, sir," Rankin said with a stoic face. "The base is under attack. The general has ordered the platoon to immediately return and assist with the defense."

Franklin looked at the warehouse and then at Ryan.

"I won't be able to stop my people." Ryan sighed deeply, then turned and walked back to his people. A ripple of alarm grew into shouts and cries as news of the departing soldiers spread through the crowd like fire through dry grass. A few civilians waved angry fists and shouted at Franklin and his soldiers. Moments later, random shots rang from the crowd and warehouse.

"Retreat!" Franklin ordered. "Rendezvous at the gas station." Then he ran to the Humvee. As he opened the door to the vehicle, most of the crowd turned toward the warehouse. Like a wave hitting the shore, the crowd tore down the fence and rolled toward the building under a hail of gunfire.

Day eleven

Portland, Oregon, Wednesday, September 14th

James stayed in the shadows as he crept through the gate and across the backyard to the garage where Emma waited. "It's me," he said into the darkness as he opened the door.

"Are they gone?" she whispered.

He shook his head but then realized she couldn't see him. "No. They've moved up the street. But I think we can get to my house."

"I saw some in uniform. Are they the good—"

"No, they can't be regular army soldiers." His foot bumped into her and he slid to the concrete floor beside her. "My dad talked about militia groups and gangs fighting for control. If we can get to my house ...." He had started to say that his dad would find them, but his father had gone on another mission and wouldn't have returned yet. "My mom will be there."

"Okay," Emma whispered. "Maybe from your house, I can get to mine. Let's go."

In his search for a way home, James had seen the mob looting homes between here and Emma's house. They were probably on her street right now, but he simply whispered, "I'll get you home."

"I found this while you were gone."

She pressed it against his hand and he took it. "What is it?"

"A flashlight. It works."

"Did you turn it on?"

"Yes, of course."

James cringed. "Someone might have seen it."

"I'm not stupid." Frustration etched her voice. "I held my hand over it and turned it on only for a moment."

"Okay." He relaxed a bit. "Still we should leave."

As they crept across the backyard, Emma asked, "Is anyone in this house?"

"No." He didn't mention the body on the front porch.

*   *   *

How many had died? As the platoon hurried back to Portland, Franklin pondered that question. How many were killed charging the fence at the distribution center, and, as he listened to Rankin describe the situation at the base, he wondered how many had died there. "Do you know who attacked? How many are there? What were their targets?"

"I can't say for sure how many are involved, but it started when a militia group attacked a weak spot in the perimeter fence." Rankin shook his head and sighed as he followed Keller's deuce along the freeway. "Hundreds, maybe thousands, of civilians followed them in and started looting homes."

"What would motivate ordinary people to assault a military installation?" a soldier in the back of the Humvee asked.

"I don't know what they wanted." Rankin sounded apologetic. "I wasn't there long before the general told me to get you guys."

"Food, I'd guess," Kohen said from the back. "You can only watch your family go hungry so long, and then you have to act."

"Even if doing something gets you *killed?*" the first soldier asked.

"I'd rather die trying to get food for my family than not act and watch them die of starvation," Kohen replied.

Franklin nodded inwardly as memories of the crowd tearing down the fence and rushing the warehouse under gunfire haunted his mind. He thought of Carol, James, and Logan, and his gut wrenched with worry. Had his own family been attacked for its meager food stock? Had they been hurt? Killed?

He knew that Private Kohen was Jewish but had never seen him read the Torah. In the last three days, he had read a half-dozen books of the Bible, including Matthew and Revelation. In those books, he had learned of the Great Tribulation, a time when the world would experience hunger and starvation. People killing for scraps of food ... was it the end of days? It felt like it.

As a military man, he had seen famine and deprivation but not in this country. He faced the reality that battling for food was preferable to watching those he loved die a lingering death from starvation.

"Just before I left, General Sattler established a perimeter around the base warehouses." Rankin turned off the freeway near the Cyber Intel Center.

"Then that is where we go," Franklin declared with more confidence than he felt. Moments later, the convoy turned down the dark city surface streets. Smoke lingered in the air, punctuated by the sound of gunfire.

Franklin scanned the nearby apartments and commercial structures for any movement as he struggled to develop a plan. A few days earlier, the general had requisitioned two buildings in that area: a large warehouse for food and the other, across the street, served as the motor pool. Both were valuable targets for capture, but food would be the most important. However, he hadn't been inside either and possessed only a vague idea of how to enter and secure them. He picked up the radio and clicked transmit. "Lieutenant Poole, have you been inside these warehouses?"

"Just the motor pool, not the food one, sir."

"You're our expert. When we get there, stay close to me."

At the edge of the base, the convoy's headlights illuminated the twisted remains of the gate scattered on the pavement along with a dozen bodies. No guards stood watch.

"Headlights off," Franklin ordered over the radio. "Sergeant Keller, use night-vision gear and don't stop until you reach the buildings."

Weaving past bodies scattered in and along the road, Keller slowed but didn't stop as the convoy proceeded under the meager light of a crescent moon. Every yard forward brought another body into view. Judging by the clothing, almost all were civilian men. Franklin shuddered inwardly. So much death.

The convoy reached the parking lot beside the motor pool and Franklin ordered the drivers to stop along the far edge near a line of trees. The soldiers poured out and gained quick cover and concealment in the darkness behind the vehicles. The black asphalt of the lot seemed to swallow the dull light that reached the ground.

Franklin exited his Humvee and, within moments, heard gravel crunch as someone raced toward him.

Poole emerged from the darkness and pointed. "That door opens to an office, break room, and hallway into the main part of the motor pool. The food warehouse is on the other side."

Franklin listened to the night. Gunfire echoed in the distance, but here there was only silence. He tried the radio. "Motor pool, this is platoon three. Over."

No answer.

Darkness would provide concealment as they advanced across the parking lot, but he wished he had more intel on the enemy and its positions. He hoped that his decisions would be wise. Adrenalin surged through him and his heart pounded. "Platoon, advance with me."

They charged into the parking area.

"Freeze!"

In the middle of the lot, Franklin stood like a statue in the open while most of his less-exposed soldiers scattered for cover. The voice was that of a woman, her forceful delivery a bark of authority from the darkness. It might be just her, or there might be a hundred people pointing guns at him and his soldiers.

"Identify yourself," the voice ordered.

"Major Dirk Franklin, United States Army." He took a deep, slow breath.

"Come forward and be identified."

"Corporal Briscoe?" Keller called to the voice. "Is that you?"

"Sarge?"

Franklin gazed at Keller and then into the darkness as he tried to put a face to Briscoe, a driver working in supply.

"I'm glad to see you guys." A young woman in ACUs led a dozen others from the darkness into the shadowy parking lot. "We just cleared this area of enemy stragglers."

Staring at the face etched by darkness, Franklin struggled to recall her first name. *Debbie? No, Dana.*

Lieutenant Poole and Sergeant Keller joined Franklin in the parking lot.

Franklin relaxed and inhaled a deep breath. "Corporal Briscoe, what's the situation here?"

"I'd call it stable. We regained control of the motor pool." Briscoe pointed at the building. "And now command the surrounding area. The remaining militia fighters are bottled up inside the food warehouse."

"Do you know the name of the militia group?"

"They call themselves the Sovereign Militia," Briscoe said. "We captured one of them."

"Good." Franklin rested both hands on his hips as he recalled Dick mentioning the group. "I'd like to talk with your prisoner, but first, where's General Sattler?"

"He's inside, sir, badly hurt. Our medic is also wounded and low on supplies."

"Medic! Bickel!" Franklin looked about. "Where are you?"

"Here, sir." She emerged from the shadows.

Along with Briscoe, Franklin led his soldiers into the building. Lanterns provided scattered circles of dim yellow light inside the large, windowless room. Near the far end, a woman huddled with two small children. Briscoe pointed to a dim corner. "The general is over there."

With one arm in a sling and a bandage around his head, the medic knelt near one of the half-dozen wounded. He held a lantern while another soldier followed his instructions. "Keep pressure there."

"General?" Franklin hurried toward the corner.

"Major?" a weak voice whispered.

Franklin knelt by his side.

Bickel ran to the other medic. "Are you okay?"

"I'll live," the wounded medic said. "So will the others, but the general … He has internal bleeding that I can't stop. We need to stabilize and transport him. Do you have an IV?"

"Yes." Bickel pulled blue gloves from her pack.

"Glad you're here," the general whispered to Franklin.

"Try not to talk, sir." Bickel checked the wound.

"Got to." The general struggled to breathe. "We figured it out too late. The attack on housing … a diversion. Burton told them about … the food."

"Burton?" Franklin tried to put a face with the name.

"Brad Burton." Poole knelt beside him. "The guy from the Multnomah County Planning Department."

Franklin shook his head in disbelief. "He told the Sovereign Militia?"

Bickel reached down with bloodstained blue gloves and inserted a needle in the general's arm, taped it down, and attached tubing. Then she passed an IV bag to a nearby soldier. "Hold this."

The general coughed blood. "Don't know who Burton told … but they found out … kidnapped his family."

When Bickel finished bandaging the wound, she locked eyes with Franklin. "He needs a hospital."

"Don't waste the time … save the food. You're going to need it." The general's eyes glazed. He shuddered and then seemed to relax with a long, slow exhale.

Bickel checked for a pulse then thrust her hands to his chest and started CPR. When sweat ran down her face, Franklin relieved her and continued chest compressions. Then Keller relieved him.

Bickel checked again for a pulse and shook her head. "I'm sorry, sir; the general's wounds … he lost too much blood." She wiped her face with a hand, smearing sweat and blood across one cheek.

His friend had been murdered by Sovereign Militia traitors. Franklin half stood before slumping into a nearby chair. He had been content as the second in command of this small intelligence center. Now General Sattler was dead and the entire situation fell to him. He wanted to find his family and run away. Where were they? Were they okay? As the adrenalin spike faded, exhaustion swept over him.

"Shouldn't there be a lot more vehicles in here?" Poole shined a flashlight around the open space. Only three Humvees, two deuces, and a fueler were visible along the back wall of the main floor.

"The Sovereign Militia attacked here and the food warehouse at the same time. They killed or wounded those on duty." Briscoe pointed a flashlight to a dark corner where twelve bodies, three in bags, lay in a line. "Then they moved most of the trucks to the other building. These vehicles were all that remained when we secured the place."

Franklin borrowed the flashlight and walked over to the bodies. Some wore standard ACUs, but instead of an American flag, they wore a crossed rifle insignia with the words Sovereign Militia below. He moved down the line of the dead to a man in a dark business suit. He had been shot, execution style, in the head. Despite the wound, he looked familiar. "Who was this man?"

Briscoe joined him. She shrugged. "He's the Brad Burton guy the general mentioned. The militia killed him during our assault on this building. That's his family over there." She pointed to the woman and two children.

Franklin pushed thoughts of the general, Burton, grieving families, and death from his mind. "Corporal Briscoe, who's the senior soldier with your platoon?"

"Ah ... Lieutenant Wesley and Sergeant Donahue are both dead, sir."

"I didn't ask that, soldier." Franklin stood and released an angry sigh. "Who is in charge here right now?"

Briscoe hesitated. "That would be me, sir."

He leaned back and raised an eyebrow. This girl, woman, was just a few years older than his son, but she had led the soldiers to secure the perimeter. She had stepped up when duty called. "Corporal Briscoe, show me the deployment of your soldiers." Franklin turned to Lieutenant Poole. "Interrogate the prisoner, and if pain is needed to make him talk, let me know."

Poole's eyes widened. "Yes, sir."

Briscoe led Franklin upstairs. "The second floor is mostly offices with windows. There's a soldier watching from each one." As they walked down the hall, checking each room, she added, "We're stretched thin, but we have the food warehouse covered."

They strode outside, crossed the dark street, and entered another building where three soldiers watched the rear of the distribution center from two windows. Inside the warehouse, a militia member peeked out through a broken window. The soldiers near Franklin sprayed the window with gunfire, shattering the remaining glass, and the traitor disappeared.

Briscoe ended the tour on the roof of a building that looked down on the main door of the food warehouse. Just as she had said, from windows and rooftops, soldiers covered every exit with multiple angles of fire.

"Good," Franklin muttered. The Sovereign Militia would pay a high price if it attempted to leave. "Did you position these soldiers?"

"Yes, sir," Briscoe said hesitantly. "Most of them."

Franklin nodded. "How many militia remain in the building?"

"About a dozen trucks fled during our assault. I don't think that many are left." Briscoe led him around the corner and back into the motor pool through a side door.

Reviewing the placement of the soldiers in his mind and Corporal Briscoe's overall disposition, Franklin knew the fight here could wait. Gunfire continued in the housing area. He turned to Briscoe and, in a voice loud enough for all the soldiers to hear, said, "You've done an excellent job, Sergeant Briscoe. You have my full confidence. Hold this position until we return."

She saluted. "Yes, sir, but it's Corporal, sir."

Franklin returned the salute. "Don't argue with me, Sergeant."

A grin widened across her face. "Yes, sir!"

"Do you have a radio?" Franklin asked.

"Yes, sir." Briscoe frowned. "The general's radio."

"What platoon are you?"

"We're survivors from several units, sir."

"Okay, I'm designating you Whiskey Team for the duration of this fight." Franklin turned to Lieutenant Poole. "Gather Alpha and Bravo Teams and get the address of every soldier here who has a local family. It's time to find our loved ones."

Hooahs resounded throughout the building.

Day Twelve

James nudged the back door of his on-base home and it squeaked open several inches. He froze. *Mom would have made sure it was locked.* With Emma beside him, he stood on the steps, trying to listen for movement inside the house, but the gunfire and shouts mere blocks away made it all but impossible. After several moments of hearing only those more distant noises, he pushed the door wide open and they tiptoed inside. "Stay by the door."

"I'd rather stay with you," she whispered.

"I don't know what's inside. Give me the flashlight."

She passed it with an angry grunt.

Leaving her behind wasn't a great choice, but taking her into a dark house where armed looters or militia soldiers might be waiting seemed like a worse option. At least at the back door she could run away from the house or into it.

Edging forward, James fingered the flashlight. Turning it on would give away his location, but it might be useful as a weapon. "Mom," he called weakly. "Logan?"

No answer returned.

He crossed the house to the open front door. When he tried to close it, he noticed the splintered latch. He held his breath. Someone had broken in.

With even greater caution, James continued searching the house. Flatware and plastic bowls were scattered on the kitchen floor. He bumped into a jar and it skidded away. *I need a light.* As the words flowed through his mind an idea took form. He found a flimsy red plastic storage lid and used a steak knife and scissors to cut a red lens for the flashlight. It cast a weak, but usable light.

The fridge door was open with nothing left inside. The MREs were gone from the pantry. A tight knot of despair settled in his gut as he checked the upstairs.

His room and Logan's looked normal, messy, but with nothing out of place. Last, he entered his parents' bedroom and recalled the storage chest in the corner. His parents never talked about it, but he knew the shotgun and ammo were stored there. He didn't know where they kept the key, but he could break in.

The latch hung open. Clothes and old blankets lay in a heap beside the chest, with the false bottom on top of it all. The gun and ammo were gone. He did a quick search around the rest of the room, and then returned to Emma. "The house is empty."

She touched his hand. "Where're your mom and Logan?"

"I don't know." He felt glad the house was dark and hid the tears that welled in his eyes. "We can rest here awhile." He pushed the couch against the front door and the two sat on the floor with their backs against it. For several moments, James didn't speak, afraid his voice would crack and reveal his fears.

Emma wept softly.

James wrapped his arm around her, drawing as much comfort from her as he tried to provide.

"Is there any food in the house?"

"No, it's all been taken."

Emma took the flashlight and walked to the kitchen. James watched as she checked every bit of the room and the pantry. She picked up a ketchup packet from the floor, opened it, and sucked out the contents.

He recalled these last few days when she had eaten every crumb of food they shared. Everyone felt hunger, but was she starving?

Emma grabbed another ketchup packet, and then another, and sucked the contents from each. When finished, she drank the last drops of pickle juice from a jar.

"Squad one, on the left," an unfamiliar voice from outside ordered. "Squad two, on the right."

Emma dropped to her knees and crawled back to James. "Could it be your father's soldiers?"

"I don't think so." James peeked out the front window. Light from a flashlight swept the yard. "They're probably part of the militia that attacked. My dad isn't supposed to be back yet. We'd better get out of here."

A vehicle rumbled down the street.

Together, James and Emma crawled to the back door and hurried into the darkness.

*   *   *

Nearly an hour passed as Franklin and his soldiers searched for their families. They found some, like Marge Sattler and Julia Gray, but mostly they encountered angry looters ransacking homes and a few militia thugs. As Franklin's soldiers pushed deeper into the housing area, the mob fought, but the militia used the darkness to hide, evade, and pull back toward the far end of the base.

Franklin jumped from the Humvee as it pulled into his driveway. He reached the porch before the vehicle stopped.

The screen door squeaked with the night breeze.

Two soldiers from the Humvee hurried to join Franklin while others combed both sides of the street.

Franklin touched the knob of the front door and it slowly moved away from his hand. "Carol!" He shoved the door against something heavy. "Carol!" With pistol in one hand and a flashlight in the other, he pressed his shoulder against the door and forced his way into the house. The couch had been moved against it. "Carol! Logan! James!"

Gunfire boomed a few blocks away, but no sound came from within the house.

Rankin and two other soldiers followed him inside. They swept their flashlights through several downstairs rooms.

"Another empty house," Rankin declared. "Where is everyone?"

Franklin ignored them and rushed to the kitchen. The door hung open on an empty fridge. A few open condiment packets and empty jars were scattered on the floor. He completed his check and hurried upstairs, taking two creaking steps at a time.

All the rooms were empty.

Where was his family? Had they survived the attack?

The storage chest in the master bedroom had been unlocked and the clothes dumped aside. The shotgun and ammo were gone. Next, he turned to the dresser where Carol had hidden a pistol beneath her underwear and bras. The lingerie had been pushed to one side and the pistol and ammo removed.

He looked around the dark room. *Carol, where are you?*

Steps sounded behind Franklin and he turned as Lieutenant Poole entered the room. "The soldiers have cleared to the end of the street. One of the scouts reported a large crowd a few blocks from here. He says it looks like two gangs are fighting near the church."

"Let's move in that direction, but clear as we go, and leave fourth squad in the rear. I don't want armed groups coming up behind us."

"Yes, sir."

Poole rejoined Bravo Troop and Franklin returned to his soldiers, but fear for his family clawed at his mind. Sergeant Keller commanded the squad on the opposite side of the street, with Lieutenant Poole on the next lane. All around him soldiers checked homes.

Midway down the block, three unfamiliar men in uniform ran from a house. Their arms were burdened with cloth bags and rifles.

"Freeze!" Sergeant Keller ordered.

One of them dropped his bag and raised a rifle.

All three men died in a storm of gunfire. Several glass jars shattered on the sidewalk while others rolled on the lawn.

Franklin walked across the street as soldiers surrounded the house.

"Seven," Keller growled.

"What?" Franklin asked.

"That's how many we have killed. Four civilians and now three militia." Keller shook his head. "The world has gone mad."

Franklin sighed. "Driven mad by hunger maybe."

They walked to the bodies sprawled on the lawn. Keller shone his flashlight on each body in turn. Darkness hid most of the blood from the wounds. He focused the beam of light where the American flag should have been on their camo uniforms. Instead, they wore the crossed rifle insignia of the Sovereign Militia. "Traitors."

"Take their weapons and ammo." Franklin stared at the house.

Keller did and pulled a radio from the vest of one of the men and passed it to Franklin. "This might come in handy."

"If it works." Franklin adjusted the squelch and it crackled with static. "And if they don't talk in code." Despite his verbal reservations, he felt better having it. "Continue clearing this street." He gestured toward the home the militia had been in. "I'll take Rankin and Kohen with me and see why these guys lingered here."

"Yes, sir." Keller motioned for his soldiers to advance.

Franklin slid the transceiver into a pocket as he entered the home, followed by the two soldiers.

In the kitchen, Franklin pointed his light at jars of home-canned food neatly stacked on the counter. He examined several containers of vegetables and meats then walked to the back porch. A greenhouse and raised garden beds still burdened with produce filled the small backyard.

Rankin approached. "Nothing upstairs." He looked out the back window. "Looks like a nice garden."

Kohen hurried toward them. "Two people shot dead in the garage, an old man and woman."

"Why kill them?" the private asked. "For the food? How did they know it was here?"

Kohen shrugged. "In better times, like those of two weeks ago, people didn't keep gardens a secret."

Franklin thought of the information Burton had provided to the militia. Were there other spies on the base? "Maybe they had a list of targets," Franklin snarled. "Let's rejoin the others."

As they exited through the front door, the militia radio crackled. "Enemy units are approaching the church. Begin phase two."

"The militia is nearby and we're being watched." Franklin looked up and down the street. "Let's get back with our people."

*   *   *

Carol Franklin looked out the broken side window of the church sanctuary. Outside, the crazed mob fought each other over scraps of food stolen from nearby homes. When the gangs had poured down her street, breaking into houses, killing, and stealing, she had decided to leave rather than fight. Many had made the same decision, but now she wondered if that had been the right choice. With only the shotgun, pistol, and the food they could carry, she and Logan had run to the church.

Where was James? She didn't know. On top of her usual concern for Dirk, she felt torn between worry for James and now Logan, curled tight under a nearby pew with his hands pressed over both ears.

When they had arrived, they found about a dozen people already there. Now nearly two hundred huddled within. Two windows to her right, a large, football lineman-looking man with dark crewcut hair used a pistol to help defend the group, but weapons were few and the mob numbered in the hundreds.

Perhaps it had been the right decision; at least they were still alive, but now a fire had started near the front of the church. On the other side of the heavy wooden doors, several men fought the growing flames in the vestibule. Smoke flowed between the doors and hung heavy in the air.

For some reason, the mob had become convinced that an enormous stash of food had been stored in the church.

A boom thundered. Shards of glass rained down beside Carol.

"Just give us the food and we'll go," someone shouted from outside.

Carol peeked out at a group of five armed men. "Don't come any closer," she muttered. "I will kill you." They kept coming and she fired the shotgun. It slammed back against an already tender shoulder.

One man screamed and they all ran for cover behind a nearby car.

Hunkered over, Pastor Duncan shuffled among the pews, praying and providing water from several canteens. "How are you doing?" he asked Logan.

"I want my dad," he whimpered.

"I've been praying that your father or other army soldiers would find us. I'm sure he'll be here as soon as he can." Hunched low, he hurried over to Carol. "How are you doing?"

She was tired, sore, frightened, and worried for her family. She didn't even want to think about the fact that she had just shot ... maybe killed, a man. She wanted to cry and give up, but for the sake of her terrified son, she couldn't ... she wouldn't. "I'm okay."

Duncan offered her water.

Carol drank several mouthfuls. "We've been hoping the mob would leave or help would come."

Duncan nodded.

"We need to be more proactive, but what can we do?"

He thought for a moment and then a grin grew across his face. "I have an idea." He hurried away toward the church vestibule.

*   *   *

The clamor of battle rattled in his ears as Franklin rushed to rejoin the platoon. Ahead on the left, Franklin spotted the old brick church. Smoke poured from the steeple like a chimney, but despite the fire, someone rang the bell again and again, but not to tell the time like it had done before. These tolls were a plea, a desperate one, for help—but from who?

Two nearby burning homes cast a yellow light over the area. Franklin stayed in the shadows as he led the others back toward the platoon. A few yards ahead, three cars had been rolled or pushed into a line. Keller hunkered down behind one vehicle, talking with a civilian woman, with a baby in her arms. The woman reached over and gently touched the bandage on Keller's face.

His wife? Kathy? No, Katie. Had she or the baby been wounded?

Guns thundered and fire crackled as other soldiers advanced by using trees, mounded flower beds, and cars. Franklin led Rankin and Kohen toward Keller and his wife.

Across the street, a civilian ran out of the shadows and into a driveway where a large silver-gray SUV sat. He held something in his hand. A gun? No. A flashlight?

The church bell rang again and again.

"Freeze," Rankin shouted.

Franklin recognized the civilian—his son, James. A blonde-haired girl followed close behind. *Emma?* They stopped for a moment and then pivoted and ran. "Hold your—"

Rankin fired.

"He's unarmed!" Franklin slapped the rifle barrel down. "James," he bellowed.

His son collapsed into the darkness between two homes. The girl slowly lifted her hands and then held a trembling pose.

The air caught in Franklin's throat. Was his son alive? His heart pounded as he ran to James. Memories of the general's slow and bloody death filled his mind. Would he relive that now with his son? A bullet tore along the sleeve of Franklin's jacket, just missing the flesh below. Without pause, he bent over to make himself less of a target and scurried on.

Tears flowed down Emma's face as she struggled to keep her hands in the air.

Franklin dashed past her, grabbed his son into his arms, and pulled the gasping boy into the firelight.

James opened his mouth but couldn't speak.

"Medic," Franklin yelled. He gazed up and down his son's slender frame but didn't see any wounds. "Are you okay?"

James opened his mouth again. Still, no sound came forth.

Kohen ran to Emma. "You can drop your arms, Miss." Then he guided her into the shadows of the building and out of the line of fire.

"Where's Bickel?" Franklin looked about but didn't see her. Rankin remained on the other side of the street. He would deal with him later. Returning his attention to his stricken son, he said, "I'm going to turn you over and look for the wound." Franklin placed one hand on his son's shoulder and another on his hip.

James pushed the hand from his hip and gulped air. "I'm ... okay." He took another breath and continued. "Fell ... knocked ... the wind ... out of me." He drew in one slow deep breath and then another. Then he sat up on an elbow and pointed. "Dad, meet Emma. She's with me."

Emma knelt beside James and Franklin.

A huge weight of worry slipped from Franklin's shoulders. He smiled at Emma. He had seen her before, but never spoken to her, and such niceties would have to wait. After a quick embrace of his son he asked, "Where are your Mom and Logan?"

"I don't know."

The worry pounced back.

"I wasn't at home when the attack happened. Emma and I have been running and hiding for over a day."

The church bell continued to toll.

Bickel ran across the dark street. "Who's hurt?"

"We're fine." Franklin looked back the way she had come. Someone lay sprawled on the lawn. "Is that Rankin?" He pointed. "What happened?"

"Shot. Dead. I've got to go." Bickel ran to the next group.

Grief for Rankin mingled with worry about his wife and young son. He looked for a relatively safe location for James and Emma and spotted it on the far side of the concrete porch behind them. "Go over there and stay low."

They'd be only a few yards away, but behind concrete and partially hidden by bushes, so Franklin felt able to concentrate on the battle.

The militia radio crackled to life. "Enemy near the church. Engaging now." He pulled out the other radio, intending to warn Lieutenant Poole, but paused. If he had one of their radios, they might have one of his. Before Franklin could figure out what to say, gunfire across the battlefield grew to a thunderous roar.

Franklin moved to the edge of the SUV. Smoke poured from the church steeple and the bell still pealed its plea for help. The squads closest to him moved to better cover and returned fire. Poole had redeployed his people to a flanking position near one of the homes.

With his wife and baby, Keller ran from the line of cars at the intersection, back toward Franklin. Together they slid behind the vehicle.

While Keller caught his breath, Franklin asked, "What's the status of your squad?"

Katie slid the wailing child under her shirt to breastfeed.

Keller nodded to Franklin and drew a deep breath. "The mob around the church isn't fighting us, but the militia is protecting them. Every time we move, they fire on us. Right now we're in a standoff."

"How many enemy combatants are in the area?"

"The militia is barricaded in those three homes." Keller pointed. "So, I can't be sure, but if they had the manpower, I think they would take us on, not just harass us."

Kohen shook his head. "The enemy has been pulling back all night, but here they're making a stand. Why?"

Franklin snorted. "Because if we're here, we can't be someplace else."

"Ah ... those other soldiers, the enemy." Katie pointed. "They told the looters that the church is where most of the food is stored and those inside are protecting it."

"Why would they say that?" Keller asked. "They know where we stored the food."

Franklin cursed. "These traitors have been several steps ahead of us for days. We need to change that." While his resolve held firm, he still needed a plan to alter the situation.

The pace of the bell tolls grew.

Franklin looked from the church to Keller and his wife. "Who's inside the church?"

They both shrugged.

Why had the militia drawn Franklin away from the food warehouse to the church at the opposite end of the base? They knew food wasn't stored there, but they told the looters that it was. The militia would likely attack the warehouse again, and soon. Protecting the food was the priority. But the ringing bell pleaded for help. Franklin gazed at the church. Billows of smoke poured from the steeple with tentacles of flame mixed in.

Kohen followed his gaze. "The families we couldn't find ... the militia ... I'll bet they pushed them here, into the church, knowing we would have to help them."

"I think you're right." Franklin swore. "We need to reach the people in the church before the fire spreads." *Please God, if my family is in there, help me save them, and everyone with them.* A plan formed in his mind. "The enemy may be monitoring our radios. Keller, tell fourth squad to reinforce Lieutenant Poole. Then tell the lieutenant to attack the militia-held homes. Our soldiers will advance on both the looters and militia."

Franklin sprinted to his son, still crouching beside the porch. He handed the wide-eyed young man a pistol. "If you need it, use it. I'll be back soon, but until I do, stay here and stay low."

"Yes, sir."

Franklin cast Emma a firm gaze. "Both of you."

She nodded vigorously.

Keller brought his wife and baby over, kissed them both, and ran off into the darkness.

Several minutes later, Kohen pointed to the street corner. "Fourth squad is moving up to reinforce Poole."

The blare of gunfire increased.

The militia radio in Franklin's pocket crackled. "Begin final phase."

Franklin pulled out his radio and pressed transmit. "Sergeant Briscoe, this is Major Franklin. You are about to come under renewed attack."

"Roger." Briscoe's voice came back to him. "I believe that has already begun."

"Good luck."

"Kohen, follow me." Franklin bent low and sprinted over to where Rankin lay. A bloody gouge tore along his neck and severed the carotid artery. Rankin had bled out in seconds—alone.

Franklin pushed anger and regret aside and grabbed the private's rifle and ammo. Then he hurried across two lawns and into the street to rejoin his soldiers. With a thud, he stopped against the door of a dark Toyota Camry.

Hunched low, Keller darted from the darkness and joined them behind the line of cars.

After several deep breaths, Franklin said, "Pass the word. Push forward to the church while we engage the militia and any looters with a weapon."

He moved to the Camry's back end. Ahead on his left, the mob clustered in several places along the side and front of the church. Off to his right, the militia hunkered in at least three homes. Franklin looked back to the church. Five men edged toward the rear of the building.

He fired two bursts.

One man collapsed to the ground, another screamed and hobbled away. The others scattered.

Like an angry clap of thunder, gunfire boomed as soldiers rushed from cover to cover. A boom drew Franklin's gaze as Bravo Troop blew open the side door of a house and rushed in.

Franklin dashed over pavement to the cover of a nearby tree. The militia rained fire on the house Bravo Troop now held. Most of the mob had fled, but a few fired from behind cars and trees at the rear of the church.

Splinters of bark flew into his face. Franklin returned fire and moved to a pickup parked near the church.

A shotgun boomed from a broken stained glass window.

"United States Army! Hold your fire!" Franklin yelled over the din of battle.

"Dirk?" A familiar voice shouted from the window.

"Carol?" He peered around the tree and, with the firelight, glimpsed her face through the broken glass.

Flames burst from the steeple and hid the cross at the peak in rolling clouds of smoke. Then, with a deafening boom, it collapsed with a final toll of the bell.

For a moment, silence reigned.

From the rubble, fire spread back along the roof of the brick building above where he had seen his wife. *Fire at the front of the building, armed mob at the rear.* He had to do something.

Franklin waved for Keller and the others to follow as he made a final dash to the church. With the butt of his rifle, he broke out the remaining glass. Wisps of smoke escaped and stung his nose.

A blanket plopped over the window frame. "Us out or you in?" Carol coughed.

The soldier beside Franklin screamed and fell to the ground.

Blood splattered onto Franklin and he wiped it from his face.

Bickel ran to the stricken man and rolled him over, revealing a chest wound.

Bullets slammed into nearby trees where men had taken cover and ricocheted off the wall near Franklin. He had hoped to evacuate those inside, but that might get them all killed by gunfire. *Gunshot now or fire later?* "In!"

He hoisted one soldier after another up to the window while the others provided cover fire.

Bickel stood and shook her head.

Franklin glanced at the dead soldier on the ground, then he helped Bickel into the church. Finally, he passed his rifle to Carol. A hand thrust out of the building. Franklin grabbed it. With the help of a large man, he scrabbled in the window and joined his men.

"Dad!" Logan scurried out from under a nearby pew and hugged his father.

Franklin bent down and wrapped his arms around the boy.

Still holding the rifle, Carol joined the embrace and kissed her husband. "Have you seen James?"

"Yes." Tears from smoke and emotion filled his eyes. "He's safe." He shone his flashlight across the sanctuary. Smoke flowed under the doors to the vestibule, like water from a flood. "How many people are here?"

"Just under two hundred," Pastor Duncan said.

A man pressed forward. "My son is missing. I need help to find him."

"My husband needs a doctor," an older woman pleaded.

The civilians pressed around the soldiers, making it difficult to move.

"Bickel, see what you can do." Franklin wiped his nose and tried to breathe through his mouth as he turned to the pastor. "There's a back door, right?"

"Yes." Duncan rubbed his eye with one hand and pointed with the other. "Two doors. We have people covering them because ...."

"I know about the shooters out back, but there's no militia," Franklin said. "The best way out is through those doors. Let's go, people."

When everyone had crowded near the rear of the church, Poole's voice burst over the radio. "Bravo Troop attacking the last enemy position."

Briscoe's voice followed. "Whiskey Troop is fully engaged."

"Roger," Franklin said over the radio. "Bravo, when done, join Whiskey. Alpha will meet you there." He told the civilians to stay away from the doors, hugged his wife and son, and then hurried back to Keller. "Lead second squad out the door on the right when I signal." Franklin pointed. "I'll take squad one out the left." When they were in position, he shouted, "Go!"

Franklin and the other soldiers burst through both doors.

Most of the mob behind the church ran. The foolish few raised their weapons to fight.

Along with several soldiers, Franklin shot first, killing eight in mere seconds.

All the others fled.

The fires cast an eerie glow through the fog-like smoke that swirled around them. Beyond the group of soldiers, the neighborhood took on a surreal, ghostly appearance. That, and the sudden silence, stunned Franklin. After several moments, he called out, "Is anyone hurt?" He spotted Bickel.

"I think we're all good, sir," she said.

"Okay, people, let's get the civilians out."

Carol and Logan were among the first to exit the church. Logan ran over and hid close behind Franklin. Carol stood next to him as people poured from the burning building. Some were helped out, hanging onto others. A few were carried out on doors or blankets tied to poles.

His radio snapped to life. "Alpha Troop, this is Bravo. We're going to reinforce Whiskey."

"Roger. We'll rendezvous with you there." Franklin turned to the soldiers and civilians with him. "Squad one on the left, two on the right, and civilians in the middle. Follow me."

Franklin led them across the church lawn as he circled back toward his son. He spotted James on one knee near where he had left him.

Emma burst from the shadows. "Dad!" She ran past Franklin and into the arms of the big man who'd helped him through the window into the church.

Still holding the pistol, James jogged over to his parents. His mother wrapped him in a hug.

"Here." Still in his mother's embrace, James passed the gun to his father. "I didn't use it."

Franklin handed the weapon to Carol. "We need to keep moving."

Briscoe's voice sounded over the radio. "Alpha leader, both warehouses are secure."

"I guess we can take a moment," Franklin said.

James mussed Logan's hair. "I'm glad you didn't get killed."

*　　*　　*

Franklin walked from the motor pool as a cold dawn spread across an angry red sky. He needed sleep, but he wanted to know how badly his people had been hurt.

His people.

He had often referred to soldiers as his people, but now the scope of those words had grown. Civilians with no connection to the military clung to them for safety.

Poole jogged out the door and handed him a list. "We have less than a hundred soldiers and over three hundred civilians. More are straggling in so those numbers will change."

Franklin stared at the page without reading.

"Twelve days." Poole shook his head. "Twelve days without food and the worst of humanity takes over."

"The worst of humanity is *trying* to take over. We will stop them."

Poole rubbed his face. "I hope we can, sir." He saluted and strode back toward the building.

Franklin walked on, looking for his family. He had read somewhere in the Bible that Light had come into the world, but men loved darkness more. He should find the book and read about the nature of good and evil. Maybe, after some rest, he would talk to Pastor Duncan.

He found Carol, James, and Logan sitting under a large fir tree with Emma and her father.

As Franklin neared, Carol stood and wiped her face, smearing soot with tears.

"What's wrong?"

"Emma's mother was killed last night during the battle."

Exhaustion swept over Franklin.

"Everything we tried to build has been burned and destroyed by fire, gangs, mobs, and militias." Tears rolled down her cheeks. "What are we going to do?"

"Tomorrow we go and find others who want to build a new world." Franklin wrapped her in a tight hug, leaned close, and kissed her forehead. "And then we start again."

*   *   *

The Storm Rises is an introductory novella to the Solar Storms Saga. See the next page for information on *Through the Storm*, book one in the Solar Storms Saga.

DON'T MISS *THROUGH THE STORM*

THE NEXT BOOK IN THE SOLAR STORMS SAGA

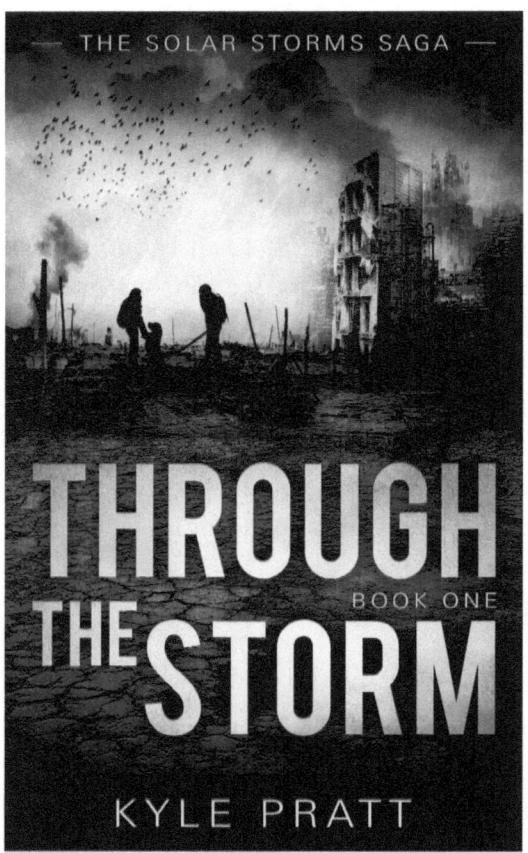

Through the Storm (The Solar Storms Saga, Book 1)

Neal Evans is in Nevada when he hears that an immense coronal mass ejection will soon slam into the Earth's magnetosphere. Will it cause only beautiful auroras to dance across the night sky or will it throw technology back a hundred years? Politicians and scientists are still debating when Neal decides to act. As night falls, Neal has ten hours to drive home before the first CME strikes.

Through Many Fires (Strengthen What Remains, Book 1)

Terrorists smuggle a nuclear bomb into Washington, DC, and detonate it during the State of the Union Address. Army veteran and congressional staffer Caden Westmore is in nearby Bethesda, Maryland, and watches as a mushroom cloud grows over the capital. The next day, as he drives away from the still burning city, he learns that another city has been destroyed, and then another. America is under siege. Panic ensues, and society starts to unravel.

About The Author

Hello, and thank you for reading.

I grew up in the mountains of Colorado and attended Mesa State College in Grand Junction. When money for college ran low, I enlisted in the United States Navy. I thought I would do four years and then use my veteran's benefits to go back to college. Life often doesn't go as we plan it.

While serving in the navy, I wrote space opera and military science fiction stories. Both *Titan Encounter* and the *Final Duty* stories fall into that period.

My first assignment was with a United States Navy unit at the Royal Air Force base in Edzell, Scotland. Two years later, while on leave in Israel, I met Lorraine from Plymouth, Devon, England. We married the next year. Together we spent the remainder of my twenty-year naval career traveling across the United States from Virginia to Hawaii and on to Guam, Japan, and beyond.

After I retired from the military, I taught in an Alaskan Eskimo village for several years while continuing to write. My first post-apocalyptic novel, *Through Many Fires*, became an instant hit, rocketing onto the Kindle Science Fiction Post-Apocalyptic list and eventually making it to the number one spot. The second book in the series, *A Time to Endure*, appeared on several genre bestseller lists and led to the recently released third book in the series, *Braving the Storms*.

Today, Lorraine and I live on a small farm in Western Washington state. You can learn more about me on my website, kylepratt.me.

If you like this story

I am an independent writer, so I don't have an advertising budget. If you've read one of my books and found it entertaining, please tell your friends. Also, the more favorable reviews a book has, the better it sells. So if you liked the story, please consider writing a review on the site where you downloaded this ebook. If you don't like the story, please tell me why.

About the newsletter

Once a month I send out an email newsletter about upcoming books, events, specials, giveaways, promotions, and more—and I give a free ebook just for signing up! Use the link below. I respect your privacy and will never rent, sell, or give away your personal information. Subscribe to the newsletter at: kylepratt.me/contact/

www.ingramcontent.com/pod-product-compliance
Lightning Source LLC
Chambersburg PA
CBHW020410130626
46549CB00006B/2502